The Doctor's Surprise Prescription

By

Roxy Wilson

Chapter One

*Just be smart enough to know when "enough is enough."
You can't complain about somebody crossing the line, if you fail
to set the boundaries. You can't complain about somebody
wasting your time, when you didn't require them to earn it...Not
everything is meant to be a "forever" kind of thing...You can't
give people too many chances to make the same "mistakes."*
~Robert Hill Sr.

The music pumping out of the speakers set the mood. Effortlessly, Layla shifted from one pose to another as her friend and photographer, Asher clicked the pictures. She'd been at it for the past three hours and was finally feeling a little drained.

"Take a break, guys," Asher stated in a commanding voice as he put down the camera.

With a sigh of relief, Layla stepped off the rug and headed for her chair. "I'm hungry."

"We've got cream of mushroom soup and some chicken salad," Asher replied as he flopped next to her. "Hey, Jo," he called to the guy responsible for the props. "Change the background and put a fan in the right corner. I want her hair to fly in the breeze." Then he turned to Layla with a smile. "It's time for you to get into a new costume, Layla."

"Give me two minutes." She picked up the bowl of cream of mushroom soup her assistant placed on the table. People thought that a model's job was glitzy and exciting. Well, it was and yet, it was also draining and exhausting.

She'd been up since five, spent two hours getting her makeup and hair done, and then spent another hour deciding on the costumes. Then after three hours of more work, she was nowhere close to done. It would be at least seven in the evening before she would be allowed to leave—but of course, Asher's pictures were always terribly attractive and glamorous—well worth the effort.

She ate quickly, aware that he sat there eagerly waiting for her to change into new clothes.

"How is Gage?" Asher asked as he checked the pictures he'd already taken on the camera.

A brief tingle of delight coursed up her spine at the mention of his name. Layla thought about her fiancé, the handsome and charming Gage Shelton. The perfect man, and although his career moved in a different path than hers, they were in sync about everything else. He was an investment banker and doing very well. "Gage is fine, doing great actually. He's due for a promotion soon, and we're finally talking about meeting his parents."

Asher scratched his cheek as he observed his assistant who was putting on a new background. "I can't believe that you guys have been together for two years, engaged for five months, and you still haven't met his parents."

Layla felt a little uncomfortable talking about Gage, but Asher was a good friend and cared about her. He didn't thrive on gossip. She could trust him. "They don't live in New York, then there's my work schedule, and his work..." She shrugged her shoulders. "It's been a pain to fix a date, but they're in town, so I'm going to see them soon."

"Do they have anything against you?" Asher lowered his voice, even though they were alone in their corner. He understood that anything she said could leak to the press and a major hoopla could be made over her words. "Perhaps, they don't approve of you?"

The spoon that she was lifting up to her mouth halted as she glanced over at one of her closest friends. Asher and she had known each other for far too long and were way too close to hide much from each other. "Gage hasn't said anything, but I guess they don't like the idea of him dating a model."

Asher grimaced. "Why? What's wrong with models?"

Layla thought about all the condemnation she'd received from various sources. Many people held models high on a pedestal, but a number of detractors existed who thought girls like her were wild and unpredictable. Some people even thought of them as ticking time bombs.

She'd heard it all before and ignored it most of the time, but sometimes it hit too close to home. This was one such incident. "We're supposed to be addicted to a number of drugs, anorexic, and high maintenance," she recounted all the terrible things that she often heard behind her back. "And that's just for starters. Anyway, his parents are old-fashioned. I get that. It's not a big deal. We're engaged, and we'll get married soon enough. All this other crap doesn't bother me."

"That's because you're beautiful and smart and he's lucky to have you in his life."

A grin crossed her lips. She put a hand on his arm and squeezed. "This is why I love you, man."

"Get a move on then, and change. I want to finish before six."

She groaned and pushed aside her bowl that was still half full. She stood. "As if that's ever going to happen. We're going to be here until at least seven, but I'll go change." She sauntered towards the changing room. When she entered the area, her gaze was drawn to the tall, stocky man who was holding a cup of cappuccino and sitting on the couch that lined against the wall. It was Bryan, her manager. "What are you doing here? I thought you left already."

Although, he wasn't required to come to the set when she was shooting, a lot of times he turned up. Bryan made her nervous. Layla was thinking about shifting to another manager, but he'd been with her for the past three years, knew the system well, and was well-acquainted with a lot of fashion designers. If she had to work without him, her life would become even tougher.

Without invitation, he ambled behind her into the changing room. "I just wanted to stick around to see if you needed me."

Layla turned to face him. "Everything is under control here. You can leave now."

Walking forward, he clasped her hand. "You're working too hard, Layla. Slow down a bit. How about I cancel your schedule for tomorrow? You can rest all day and we can go out for dinner."

Ever since she announced her engagement with Gage, Bryan's attitude underwent a significant change. He'd become clingier and even a tad bit lecherous. "Don't be silly, Bryan. I can't afford to cancel my work at a day's notice. This is a cutthroat industry. I'd be laughed out of work in no time." She tugged her hand free. "And as a matter of fact, you know quite well that I'm engaged. How can I go out with you for dinner?"

He smiled, but to Layla it seemed somewhat forced. "Gage doesn't pamper you enough. A woman like you needs more attention."

"He gives me enough time." She hated discussing this with him. "And in any case, my personal life is none of your business."

Much to her astonishment, he put a hand on her shoulder and squeezed. "We're friends, aren't we? It's not just a professional relationship. I care for you, Layla."

She opened her mouth to speak.

Asher barged in. "Hey, man. Go back to your cappuccino already. Layla has work to do."

Bryan snarled, but removed his hand. After throwing a fulminating glare towards Asher, he marched out of the room.

Unperturbed, Asher closed the door behind him. Walking over to the rack that contained all the costumes, he pulled out one. "Wear this, baby girl. You'll look great in it."

Even though she was still disturbed by Bryan's attitude, Layla took the full-length, boysenberry-colored gown from Asher's hand. "Thanks."

"No problem." He understood that she tacitly referred to his intervention with Bryan. "You know sooner or later, you will have to get rid of that guy." Asher crossed his arms, even as he narrowed his eyes. "He's got his eyes on you, and not in a good way. You've got to break ties before he crosses the line."

She winced. Layla hated confrontations. It was one of her biggest nightmares. "I don't know how I can do that. Perhaps he's just being—?"

"Obnoxious? Creepy? I think those are the words that you're looking for."

He was right, of course. She couldn't tolerate this kind of behavior anymore. It was time to put her foot down and get rid of this man who made her nervous. She was actually scared to be alone with Bryan now, and in a professional relationship, she couldn't afford to be like that.

Absentmindedly, she picked up the hairbrush that lay on the counter and ran it through her hair as she contemplated Asher's words. "I'll do it." A thin strip of hair fell on the floor at her feet. Layla stared at it without understanding the significance of such an event.

Asher spared a glance for the coil of hair and then waved his hand. "Do it soon, baby girl, or it's only going to get worse," he emphasized as he opened the door and stepped out. "I'm waiting." He glanced pointedly at his watch. "Tick tock."

Layla sighed. She strolled over to the door and locked it before anyone else could come in. It was important to take a few minutes to be alone once in a while. She quickly changed and then checked her makeup in the mirror. Her hair, blackberry colored hair, hung down her back, her espresso brown skin glowed. Her deep, brown eyes that stared back at her were bright and alert despite the fatigue that'd set in.

She knew she was beautiful...indeed, she'd heard it often enough. The product of mixed genes, her features were strangely attractive and her figure was hourglass.

She felt lucky to have found a job in the modeling industry which gave few chances. Even though Layla enjoyed her work, lately she had been feeling a bit tired of the same humdrum routine.

Maybe it's time to switch gears and do something else, but she didn't have the courage to take the plunge. If she left this industry for as much as a week, someone else would take her place.

Layla was on her way to making a good name for herself. Already well-known in her neck of the woods, but she was aiming to become a supermodel in her own right. Or, she should say that's what her mom wanted her to aim for. If she told the truth, Layla didn't harbor that same desire.

Perhaps once she proved herself, she would be able to sit back on her laurels and enjoy her life a bit. Right now, it was all about work, but maybe she would be able to relax a little when she made it to the top.

A pipe dream of course. The busier and more productive her life became, the more she felt as if she rode a merry-go-round from which she couldn't get off. She kept doing the same things over and over again, with no chance for escape. "No point complaining, girl. This is what you do, and you're damn good at it," she said to her reflection in the mirror. "Let's go out and finish this job."

Once she strode out, Layla felt relieved to see that Bryan wasn't outside anymore. Perhaps he felt embarrassed by Asher's attitude and left. *Good!* She couldn't bear to deal with him right now. She strolled back into the room where the shoot was going on.

When she stepped on the rug once more, Asher smiled. "Looking good, baby girl. Now, I want you to look a little pensive. Give me your sad face."

Without much effort, she arranged her expression so that it suited his instructions. It wasn't too difficult for her to shift from pose to pose. Layla was good at her work, and she had to admit, there were times when she still enjoyed aspects of it.

After 2 more changes of costumes and four hours of hard work, she rushed out of the studio. She practically jogged over to the nearest subway station.

As much as she was able to, Layla preferred to live a normal life. Once she reached home, she took a hot shower. Her body felt so tired, but her mind was still active. As she reached forward to take the bar of soap that was created in the shape of a teddy bear, a smile broke over her face. In her free time, she liked to create different types of soap.

Her dream was to start her own brand of soap and market it on a national level. Of course, this was a distant goal. She wouldn't be able to dump her work and do whatever the hell suited her. First, she would have to set aside enough savings— oh well, she probably had enough of that. Second step was to reduce her assignments, but that would probably kill her career. She wasn't quite ready to do that.

Maybe, someday, she would do the thing that her heart really wanted.

On impulse, she decided to give her hair a brisk shampoo. Being a woman of color, it wasn't practical to wash her hair every day, but tonight was an exception. She squeezed a dollop of shampoo on her palm, rubbed it in with both hands, and massaged it onto her scalp.

Oooh, it felt good! The scent was great too. It made her feel as if all the stress and tension of the day were dissipating. When she'd rubbed the shampoo onto her hair completely, she stood beneath the water, mindful to keep her eyes closed. She then finished rinsing her hair.

Blindly, she reached for the soap and lathered her skin, once again. Gingerly, she opened her eyes, wincing a bit as she felt the slight burn. Damn it, she always managed to get a bit of it in her eyes anyway. When she rubbed the soap over her body, her gaze was drawn to the clumps of hair, as thick as her thumb, pooling at her feet and moving towards the shower drain. The horrified gasp that escaped her lips was nothing in comparison to the fear that coursed through her veins.

What was going on?

Why did so much of her hair come off?

It wasn't the first time she'd used that brand of shampoo. And besides, it always left her hair looking beautiful. She reached out and grabbed her towel, wrapped it around her body, stepped out of the shower and rushed in front of the mirror, her heart beating rapidly. She raked her fingers through her hair

A wave of nausea overcame her. Wet strands of her hair were stuck to her fingers. More fell into the sink.

Did she have some terrible disease?

Cancer?

Lupus?

Was she going to die?

The faces of some of her family members rushed through her mind. Her maternal grandfather was bald, and even some of her uncles were balding, as well. But what about the female members of her family? As far as she could tell, none of them were losing hair, except for an aunt who'd fought breast cancer with the resultant radiotherapy and chemotherapy for a number of years until she lost the battle a year ago.

Layla couldn't afford to lose her hair. It was her crowning glory.

She shook her head. She refused to believe she was terminally ill.

Is it stress?

The situation with Bryan was really stressing her out, and her career was very demanding. Yes, yes, yes. Some people reacted differently to acute stress. Some lose weight. Others gained weight. She even remembered one of her model friends developing bad acne because of stress. Maybe, she needed to pick up yoga as a stress-relieving activity. Maybe it was because of her diet. She could be allergic to something she'd been eating and didn't even realize it.

Yes, that's it. Now, she would definitely have to start being more disciplined about keeping a food journal to record all the things she ate each day. As a woman, and a model, it would be devastating for her to walk around with a baldhead.

She glanced at the mirror again.

What the hell is happening to me?

Chapter Two

I may not be perfect, but I don't need to be. Take me as I am or watch me as I walk away. ~Unknown

A week later, desperate to find some answers, Layla stepped into the hospital. If she didn't figure out the reason why her hair was falling out, she might lose her career. She couldn't afford to do that. Hence, she didn't waste any time in setting up an appointment.

Beside her, Asher pulled a face. "Why do I have to be with you?"

She held up the bag of Subway cookies that he was so fond of. "Because you love these."

He took the bag from her and dug out a cookie as they headed for the reception. "I love you," he muttered.

Touched by his sweet comment, she put her hand on his arm even as she handed the receptionist the paperwork that was already prepared by her doctor. "I'm here to get some tests done."

The nurse read through her file. "We'll take your history, ma'am." She turned and pointed to a closed door on her right. "Please wait in that room and someone will be along to ask you some questions. He'll then escort you to the lab for tests."

While she turned towards the waiting room, Layla's eyes were drawn to the charts and words that were put up everywhere. Oncology. Could she have cancer? Her doctor assured her that her hair loss could be due to some simple reason, but she couldn't help but wonder if she might be dying.

Was she destined to lose it all when she'd worked so hard to come this far?

Is this the end of her journey?

Would she spend the last days of her life in the hospital, alone and miserable?

Layla shuddered as she took a seat.

Asher crunched down on another cookie. "This place depresses me," he announced.

"Me, too," she confessed.

He glanced at her, perhaps understanding the fear on her face and put his arm around her. "Don't worry, baby girl. It's going to be all right. Nothing is going to happen to you. It's probably some sort of vitamin deficiency or something like that."

She'd told him about the reason for the tests that she was required to undergo. She'd assumed that he would be horrified, but he assured her it wasn't the end of the world. "What if it isn't? What if this is permanent?" she worried.

"I've already told you that it doesn't matter. You can work just as well with a wig, or hair extensions, or hats. There are a number of accessories that can make this thing disappear."

"It wouldn't just disappear. I would have to cover it up all the time. People will know."

"And they wouldn't care. All they want is for you to look good on the ramp or on the cover of a magazine, and if you can manage that, ninety percent of your job is done."

Layla wasn't quite sure. Asher was just trying to make her feel better. She couldn't bear it if she lost her contracts because of this new problem.

For years, she'd been working hard to chart out her career and now, to lose it because of her hair loss, would be devastating. Just as she opened her mouth to ask him if he really thought this hiccup wouldn't affect her career, his cell phone rang.

"Hello." He sat up straighter, the bag of cookies forgotten in his hand. "Okay, I'll be there in 45." He put the phone back in his pocket and stood. "I'm sorry, but I have to go."

"What happened?"

"One of my assistants got into a car accident. They took him to a hospital, and I should go—but maybe I can come back in a little while..."

"Don't worry about it. I'll be fine."

He looked hesitant to leave her alone. "Maybe you can postpone this until I can come back with you?"

It was sweet of him to offer, but she didn't think she would have the courage to go through this again. She was here now, and it would be better to get it over with. "I'll be fine. Seriously, just go."

He strode out, just as a doctor marched in. "Ms. Turner?"

"Yes, that's me." She waved to Asher to assure him again that she was fine.

The doctor settled down in front of her and balanced a clipboard on his knee. "Ma'am, I would like you to answer some routine questions before we take you in for some tests."

Layla trembled a bit; she was scared of needles. "What kind of tests?"

"Nothing major. Some blood tests." When she winced, he smiled. "Don't worry. It will be painless."

Yeah, right! She sighed as she prepared herself for some pokes. It wasn't going to be easy, but as long as they diagnosed her and gave the right treatment, she was game to try anything. Quickly, she answered his questions. Regarding her father's history, she fumbled. "I'm afraid I don't have any information on my paternal family. I never met my father."

He didn't appear perturbed by it. "It's okay, ma'am."

Moving on, they filled in the rest of the questionnaire. Once they were finished, he signed at the end. "This is good. Why don't you fill in your insurance information over here while I set things in motion?"

When he strolled away, she leaned back against the seat and began to fill in the rest of her paperwork. Layla didn't like to think about her father. He was a dark secret that she liked to hide. As she pondered over the missing piece of her medical history and the implications of it on her condition, her attention was drawn to a little girl who sidled into the room and leaned against the wall as if she was hiding from someone. Layla expected an adult to come in after her, but when no one walked in after five minutes, she cleared her throat.

The girl jumped. No more than eight or nine, she looked terrified. Her gaze settled on Layla. It seemed as if she'd been crying.

Layla didn't have a lot of experience with young children, but this one looked as if she needed a bit of attention. "Are you okay, dear?"

The girl gulped. Her gaze darted to the door as if she was contemplating running away. She bit her bottom lip hard.

Surely, someone must be looking for her. Layla didn't want her to slip out. It was better to keep her occupied until someone came in to take her. "What's your name?"

"Charlotte."

"That's a beautiful name." She smiled.

The girl was very pretty. Her short, wavy, champagne-blonde hair was styled in the quadruple twist and her cherubic face looked angelic.

"Why don't you sit here with me, Charlotte, until your mommy comes?"

"I don't want to go to the doctor." Charlotte's lips trembled and tears poured out of her denim-blue eyes. "My hair falls out every time they give me medicines."

A well of sympathy poured into Layla's heart. Was the girl a patient in this ward? It was quite likely that she was undergoing radiation therapy. "My hair is also falling out," Layla confessed before she had time to wonder as to why she felt comfortable talking to this child when it was so hard for her to discuss the same subject with her doctor. "See. I will show you."

After a moment of hesitation, the girl walked closer.

When she was a mere three feet away, Layla took off her hat and bent her head to show her the bald patches on her scalp.

It was obvious to see that the child had lost more than half her hair. No wonder she was scared. "It looks bad," the girl whispered in a candid voice. "Does it hurt when it comes out?"

"No, it doesn't. Does yours hurt?"

"Only when they give me medicines." She sighed. "I don't want to come to the hospital anymore."

Layla stood. Someone had indeed misplaced this child, and it was important to take her back. Moments ago, she was dreading the next step she needed to take in the hospital, but now she was filled with a newfound purpose. "I know, dear. Even I don't like hospitals and medicines, but we have to do it because if we don't, we won't get better. You do want to be healthy, don't you?"

The girl stared at Layla for a moment before she nodded. "I do."

"Good then. Let me take you to your mommy and the doctor and they can give you the medicines that will make you strong." Bending down, she wiped the tears from the child's cheeks. "Can I tell you a secret?"

"What?"

"I'm as scared as you," she said. "Maybe together, we can be strong."

Much to her surprise, the child slipped her fingers into Layla's hand. "Okay, then."

Together, they marched out of the room.

Layla didn't have a clue as to where she needed to take the child. Perhaps she could ask the receptionist.

Just as they stepped towards the reception, a doctor came sprinting down the stairs. "There you are, Charlotte. We've been looking all over for you."

My, oh my! This was some eye candy. Layla wasn't often impressed with a man's looks, but his warm, Espresso-colored eyes and the friendly smile on his face made her heart pound in her chest. Forgetting her own woes, she stared at him as if he were an angel sent from heaven.

His gaze focused on her and narrowed as he saw her holding the girl's hand. "Hi. My name is Clint. Dr. Clint Collins. Did you find her?"

"Actually...she found me." Layla finally found the words that were stuck in her throat. "I was sitting in the waiting area when she came in."

"Ah! Come on, Charlotte. We've been waiting for you."

In response, the girl hid behind Layla. "I don't want to go."

Once more, her heart squeezed in sympathy at the young child's plight. It couldn't be easy to be stuck in this place where everything looked scary and hostile. "You want me go up with you, Charlotte?"

The girl nodded.

Layla straightened.

The doctor kept eyeing her with a speculative gleam in his eyes. "She seems to trust you. Come along then. It's time for her treatment, and her mother is a bit agitated."

Layla held the child's hand as they climbed up the stairs.

The pediatric oncology department occupied the first floor.

A tall woman, with auburn hair, was pacing the floor. "Charlotte, it was naughty of you to run away." Seeing her daughter's hand in Layla's, she frowned. "Who are you?"

Layla introduced herself. "Charlotte and I have become friends, haven't we?"

"We have," the girl confirmed. She didn't let go of Layla's hand. "Will you wait for me while I go inside?"

"Sure." Layla bent to give the child a hug. Her delicate, small body seemed fragile, but the rosy flush on her cheeks indicated that she wasn't doing so badly. "Good luck!"

When Dr. Collins held out his hand, the girl took it. She strolled inside with him while Layla took a seat.

"She doesn't like coming to the hospital," her mother admitted. "But if she doesn't get the treatment, she won't get well."

Layla nodded. Sure, it was necessary but it seemed obvious the child needed more reassurance than what her mother was capable of giving. Perhaps she was being unsympathetic. It couldn't be easy to see her child go through such a nightmare. Rather than ask any questions, Layla sat and waited for Charlotte.

The mother took out a phone and began to type out some messages.

Layla could have easily left now that the girl was inside, but she did promise Charlotte that she would wait and she didn't feel like breaking her promise.

A couple of hours later, Dr. Collins appeared with the girl.

She was seated in a wheelchair and looked much weaker.

Layla bit her bottom lip as she gazed at the child's pale cheeks. The radiation appeared to have sucked out all her energy.

The mother stood. She bent to give her a hug. "Ready to leave?"

The child nodded, but her eyes sought Layla. Seeing her, she smiled.

Layla went forward and patted the child's hand. "You were brave, weren't you?"

"I was."

"Soon, it shall be over, okay? And you will be as well as all your other friends."

The mother took the wheelchair and led her out but not before Layla saw the beautiful smile on the child's face. Once they left, she sighed. It was time to get on with finding a solution to her problems. Much to her consternation, the doctor was still there, looking at her with a mixture of curiosity and admiration.

"You're very good with children. Are you a teacher?"

She shifted on her feet, feeling awkward by the attention he gave her. "Actually, I'm a model."

"Really?" he blinked in surprise. "Well, you're definitely beautiful enough to be one."

The compliment threw her off. She was used to men coming on to her, but the sincerity that reflected in his eyes told her he actually meant what he said. "Thank you." She took in a deep breath and then let is out slowly. "I should go..."

"Are you visiting someone?"

"I'm here for some tests, and I was supposed to wait downstairs."

Belatedly she remembered that she might have missed her chance to go to the lab. As if he understood her predicament, the doctor held out his hand.

She handed him her papers. He studied them. She felt a little self-conscious as his gaze moved over her chart. What is he thinking? Would he still think she was beautiful when he realized she was fast becoming bald?

And why the hell did she care about what he thought?

Sure, he was handsome but so were a lot of other men she met. Her world was full of good-looking men, and she was never swayed by their physical appearance or charm. But there was something different about Dr. Collins. He was a good soul. Layla was amazed at her own assessment. She didn't even know the man, but somehow it was easy to read the sheer goodness that radiated out from him.

"I'll take you to the right department."

She followed him as he led her up another flight of stairs. It was kind of him to show her the way when he could have just as easily told her where to go.

He stopped in front of a door. "This is it. Just go inside, show them your papers, and they will deal with the rest." He smiled. "Would you like me to come with you?"

She took the papers from his hand and sucked in a deep breath of air. If that little girl could be brave, so could she. Charlotte was battling cancer whereas she was merely dealing with hair loss. It was kind of him to offer. "Thank you. I'll manage."

"Layla," he said as she stepped towards the door. "That's your name, right?"

"Yeah." She tucked a lock of her hair behind her ear. "It is."

"It's highly unethical of me to—do this, but I was wondering if you would like to go out with me sometime?"

She blinked her eyes. Did he just ask her out? "I'm engaged," she blurted out.

"Ah! Well, never mind then." He waved a hand.

For some strange reason, she felt bereft as if she had committed some major blunder but the truth was that she felt committed to Gage. Even if she weren't, this wouldn't be a good time to embark on a new relationship. Given what she was going through, she needed a lot of support and that could only be given by someone who loved her. Gage was that man, and not this stranger.

"Good luck," he said before striding back from where he came.

Layla felt bad about turning him down. He seemed sweet and eager, but she loved Gage. She watched the doctor walk away, and then with a final fortifying breath, she opened the door and stepped inside to face her demons. Whatever happened next, she planned to deal with it the same way she dealt with everything else in her life; and that was with aplomb and confidence.

Life might throw a bunch of problems her way, but she intended to be strong enough to deal with them. Nothing could faze her. She was as steady as a rock, now and always.

Chapter Three

You don't have to be anyone other than who you authentically are, and you sure as hell don't have to spend your time and energy trying to convince people that you're worth keeping around. ~Daniell Keopke

Layla resisted the urge to adjust her hat as she sat in the restaurant with her future parents-in-laws. This would be their first meeting and she hoped they would be able to get past this awkward space and move into a better future.

It didn't help that the looks they gave her were full of ire and suspicion. What did they expect her to do? Did they think she was going to throw a tantrum in public or perhaps break into her signature moves? Rather than say something mean or derogatory, she curbed the impatience that bubbled in her heart and smiled sweetly at them. "Shall we order?" She accepted the menu from the waiter. "They have a wonderful variety of seafood."

"I don't like seafood," Gage's mother sniffed haughtily.

"They have other things too," she said quickly. Why the hell were they behaving like this? What did she ever do to them? Layla was surprised that Gage couldn't see the open hostility that emanated from his parents. Or perhaps, he was deliberately ignoring it.

Gage's father wrinkled his brow as he read the menu. "Pretty pricy place."

"It's all right, dad. Just order what you want."

"We never taught you to throw money away like this," his mother sneered.

"It's not wasting, mom. We're celebrating."

"What are you celebrating? Have you set a date for the wedding as yet?" The look on his mother's face clearly told her this news wouldn't be taken well.

"It's the first time you've met Layla. I think it calls for some kind of a celebration." Gage smiled. He didn't look perturbed by their rude behavior. Perhaps this was normal in their family.

Layla wasn't sure if she felt the slightest bit comfortable with this development. She'd always known that his parents didn't like her, but this was downright humiliating.

"Hmph." His mother snorted. "I'll have the steamed chicken with oregano and mustard."

Gage put aside his menu. "Sweetie, can you please order the beef for me?" He rose from his seat. "Excuse me. I'm going to the washroom."

Layla felt this terrible urge to yank him back into his seat. She didn't think it was possible for her to survive alone with his parents for even a few seconds. When he left, she smiled at them and glanced at the menu again, as if she was ready to memorize it.

"You do know that this isn't going to work out," his mother hissed the words.

Layla glanced up, not sure if she heard correctly. "What do you mean?"

"It might look all good now, but when…*if*…you get married, he wouldn't be able to tolerate the kind of lifestyle that you lead. Women like you, the ones who flaunt their bodies and lure men, are not really his type. I don't know what he sees in you," his mother muttered hatefully. Her gaze darted in the direction her son had wandered off to as if she wanted to say everything before he came back. "It's a mistake, and the sooner you realize it, the better it is for everyone."

It was almost as if she was punched in the face. Never before did anyone talk to her in such a manner. The woman must be insane, and probably her husband too, because he stared at Layla as if he agreed with everything his wife said. So, they didn't like her. *Big deal.* She could live with that because Gage loved her. If it were anyone else, she would've given them a piece of her mind, but Layla swallowed the anger threatening to engulf her. "You don't know me, Mrs. Shelton. If we got to spend some time together, you'll realize that I'm not such a bad person."

"It's not about being good or bad, although how you can excuse away your shameless behavior with such ease, I'll never understand...You don't fit into my son's life, and you'll never be accepted into our family."

Just as Layla opened her mouth to speak, Gage slipped into his seat. "What's going on?"

"Nothing," Layla said quickly.

His mother put her hands on the table. "I'd decided early on, not to talk about it in the open, but I've now come to the realization that some things need to be said out loud."

"Mother," Gage protested.

"You don't want me to speak about it. I understand." She raised a hand to silence her son. "But I feel that I must tell her what to expect if she marries you. We, your father and I, are not happy with this decision. You've rushed into it, and I'm afraid that it's going to end badly."

Layla glanced at Gage, sure that he was going to tell his mother off any moment now. So, he was well aware that his parents didn't like her. He hid that fact from her probably, because he didn't want to hurt her. Now, she finally understood why she never saw them before. But this was crazy. They couldn't insult her so openly and expect to remain on good terms with Gage. Surely, he would tell them off. This wasn't fair. She hadn't done anything to them, and yet they continued to harass her.

Gage glanced away. Rather than say something, he just looked in another direction as if he couldn't even hear his mother's humiliating words.

"You shouldn't get married," his father added.

Layla couldn't take the insults anymore. What the hell was going on here? The man she counted on to protect her, to stand in front of her like a shield, was actually looking the other way as if he couldn't even hear the conversation.

Although there was a lot that she could have said to shut them up, she didn't want to make matters worse by opening her mouth. They accused her of being below their expectations, but it was actually they who failed their son.

And Gage failed her.

She stood up. "I'm leaving." She straightened her spine, stared all of three of them down, one at a time, then spun around, and waltzed off.

Gage marched behind her. "Layla, listen. I know they're not talking sense, but just bear with me. Ignore what they're saying."

She whirled to face him. The quick movement made her fashionable hat tip, and as she captured it with her hand, Layla was well aware that the bald patches on her head were clearly visible for a few seconds.

The horrified look on Gage's face told her that he didn't miss anything.

The murmurs that started among the people who were sitting closest to them told her that some of them saw it too. She glanced back towards the table where his parents were sitting. The open hostility on their face made her feel even more demoralized. Humiliated, she forgot what she was about to say. She rammed the hat back down on her head. "I should go."

Gage reached her before she could hail a cab on the street. His hand clasped around her arm. "What the hell is going on here? Your hair—it's..."

"It's falling out. I went to the hospital a few days ago to do some tests. They don't know...but they're doing everything to find out the reason behind it."

Letting go of her arm, he crossed his arms over his chest. "Why didn't you tell me?"

"I wanted to do so after I knew something more about it. This isn't the right time to talk about that."

"So when is the right time? After you've made all the decisions?"

"Don't talk to me like that. You're the one who sprung that surprise on me. We've been seeing each other for two years. It might have been better if you'd told me at some point that your parents didn't like me. At least, I would've been prepared."

"What did the doctor say about the hair loss?" he asked as if he didn't hear her accusations.

She couldn't believe that they were still talking about it as if she hid something monstrous from him. He was the one she needed to lean on and instead, he glared at her in an accusatory manner, as if she committed some grave error. "The doctors don't know anything as yet."

When she stomped away, he made no attempt to follow her.

Layla felt as if her world just collapsed around her. First her hair, then Gage's parents, and now—him. What else did she have to endure before this nightmare came to an end? She hated it. It was terrible to feel that no one loved her enough to offer her some level sympathy, to gather her in their arms, and tell her that everything was going to be all right.

She wanted Gage to do that. He was supposed to be her rock, but instead he was more worried about his parents and about the implications of her hair loss on his life.

It's just the shock, she decided. Surely, he felt devastated *for* her but couldn't express himself. She didn't tell him, and perhaps that's why he was upset.

Only once she was home did she allow herself to let loose the tears that pooled in her eyes.

Couldn't she get a break anywhere?

What the hell was going on in her life these days?

Everything seemed to be falling apart, and she didn't quite know how to put it back together. When she closed her eyes, much to her surprise, the image that floated up to the top of her thoughts was of the handsome Dr. Collins. Layla opened her eyes in a flash. Why would she think about that man? She didn't even know him…yet, somehow, she felt that if he was around, he would've been able to offer some comfort.

Layla fell into an uneasy sleep, and when she woke up in the morning, she was greeted by the sight of more hair piled on top of her pillow. The sight triggered fresh tears to spring to her eyes. While mourning the loss and wondering if the doctors would soon get to the bottom of this mystery, her cell phone rang.

It was Gage.

She picked up. "Hello."

"Layla, what's going on with you? You're going through something terrible, and you didn't even mention it to me."

Layla picked up a lock of her hair and curled her fist around it. No good morning. No declarations of love. Instead, he launched straight into an argument. "I didn't want to tell you before I knew for myself what was going on."

"Is it a disease?"

"I don't know, Gage. I've no idea what it is."

"How long has it been going on?"

"A week or two, I guess."

He let loose an expletive. "You've known about it for weeks, and yet you didn't tell me!" She heard him exhale a deep, gush of breath. "Look, Layla. I don't think this is going to work out."

She felt too distressed to make sense of his words. "What isn't going to work out?"

"I need some time to rethink this decision."

She still didn't get it. "Which decision?

"About us getting married."

It felt as if a truck rolled over her. Where was the sympathy she expected? Where were the quiet mummers that everything was going to be all right? She wanted him to soothe her, calm her, but instead he was stepping away as if she were a leper—and right after she tolerated the humiliation that his parents piled on her lap.

Another woman might have yelled and cursed, but she was too overwhelmed to talk. "Fine, Gage. Call me when you know what you want." She hung up.

Would she ever hear from him again?

Would he come back?

She didn't have a clue. All she knew was that this man wasn't the one she got engaged to. Gage, the one she loved, was always kind and loving. This man only seemed to be concerned about his thoughts, his needs, his image. She didn't like it.

Not one damn bit.

Layla took a bath and slipped into a pair of jeans and a royal-blue cami. She felt too drained to give more thought to Gage and his horrible behavior. Perhaps she made a mistake by not telling him, but this wasn't the kind of response she expected. While she pondered over the possible implications of his behavior, the doorbell rang.

Without thinking, Layla opened the door.

Her mother breezily strode in without looking at her. "Good morning, darling. It's been a while, so I thought I should drop in to take a look at you. You're so busy with your life that you've forgotten about me."

"That's not true, mom." She wanted to run into the bedroom and cover her head with a scarf, but it was too late.

Her mother already turned towards her. "I tried to call you two days ago, but your phone was switched off. I was—" Her mouth fell open, and the high-pitched scream which emanated from her lips pierced the air. She pointed at Layla's head, ran forward, and grabbed her shoulders. "What's wrong with your hair?"

She glanced down at her mother who was almost a foot shorter than Layla's almost 6-foot frame. "It's falling out."

"Falling out? What do you mean?" she shrieked.

This wasn't a good idea at all. Layla wished she could've kept her predicament from her mother for some time. Mary, her mother, never reacted positively to any change. She wouldn't take it well. "I've been to the doctors already, mom. They're trying to find out the reason behind it."

Her mother's hand flew to her chest. "Your hair. Your beautiful hair!" Her slate-gray stare looked incredulous. "What—" Mary shook her head, as if her brain was not processing what she saw with her own eyes. "How—"

Layla's gaze traveled to her mother's hair which was exactly the color of hers. Or had been when Layla boasted a head full of hair. It was the one thing she'd inherited from her mother. Actually, it was the only thing they had in common.

Now...it was disappearing.

Mary wasn't going to take it well, as evidenced by the color virtually draining from her apricot-colored skin. When she collapsed on the couch, prostate with grief, Layla sat next to her to offer her some consolation. Once more, she was struck by the strangeness of this situation. Mary should have comforted her, but it was the other way around. "It's going to be okay, mom. I'm sure they'll find a cure for this."

"Is it a disease?"

She winced at the same question Gage asked. "They're not sure as yet. It will take time before the doctors find some answers, but I have to go back to the hospital soon."

Her mother hunched on the couch. "I should stay over here until all this is sorted out."

Layla didn't think it was a good idea. Mary could be a hyperactive, controlling woman who was ridden with anxiety. Her mind had long ago deteriorated and all she could spout were lists of fears and caution. She wasn't a good influence on Layla and living with her would bring to life all the doubts Layla managed to suppress or deal with ever since she became independent, when she turned 18 six years ago. "Mom, I'm fine."

"You're not," Mary stated as she stood up. "I'm going to bring my stuff and stay here in case—anything happens to you. It's not good to be alone at a time like this."

At a time like what? She wasn't sick... not really. And she wasn't dying. What did her mom think was going on? "I'm fine, mom. You don't need to turn your life upside down for me."

"I insist." Mary sniffed. "Do you have sherry? I need to calm my nerves after the shock I just had."

The shock she just had? Layla was the one going through shit, but there would be no point arguing with her mother. She was like a force of nature. Once she settled on a course of action, nothing could deter her. "I'll get some for you." She went into the kitchen, took out her bottle of sherry and a glass.

Mary came in. "Never mind, dear. I'll manage myself. Why don't you go and rest?"

Layla checked her watch. She was running a bit late. Mary's unexpected visit threw her off her schedule. Just because she was suffering from hair loss didn't mean she could ditch her assignments. "I actually need to go to work, mom."

She hoped her mother would take the hint and leave but she poured a glass of sherry. She took a delicate sip and shuddered. "Go ahead, dear. I'll be right here when you come back. It shouldn't take me that long to gather my stuff, and don't worry about letting me in or anything. I have the spare key of your apartment at my place. When I come back, I'll use it to get in."

Layla resisted the urge to bang her hands on the counter. Frustration bubbled through her. She loved her mother, but the woman sure could get on her nerves. If they had to stay together for long, she would probably end up saying something that would start World War III, but this wasn't the time to argue with her mother. When she was on a mission, nothing could stop her.

"Take care, mom." She kissed her on the cheek and hurried into her room. After putting on her hat, she picked up her purse and phone. Once she got out, Layla took a deep, fortifying breath. The situation would resolve itself soon. At least, that was her hope. Mary's presence was likely to make her life even more problematic. She wasn't a calming influence at all.

When she got to the studio, Layla was faced with another problem. "This just wouldn't do," said Francis, the hairdresser, as he examined her. "I can't work with this. Your hair is a mess. You'll have to wear a wig."

Tears stung at the back of her eyes but she pushed them back with a force of will. It wasn't as if she created this situation. "Do you have one at hand?"

"Yeah. But I think we should cut your hair and make it really short for now. That way a wig will fit easily and you can wear it all the time."

Layla didn't like it, but the idea made sense. The bald patches were now all too obvious. She couldn't even hide them, and it wasn't practical to wear hats all the time. After remembering what happened in the restaurant, she thought it was a better idea to wear a wig instead. Her heart clenched as she pondered over this dilemma. Cutting off her hair was a huge thing but under the circumstances, it was the ideal solution. "Go ahead."

Even though Layla was aware of the low murmurs that continued when he began chopping off her hair, she didn't bother to check to see who might be talking.

Naturally, the news regarding this would spread far and wide. Gossip traveled at the speed of lightning in the modeling industry. People thrived on it. Her competitors were bound to have a big laugh over this, but she couldn't allow them to bring her down. She would fight this till the end.

After being fitted with the wig and the makeup done, Layla walked to the set to start the photo shoot. Much to her surprise, no one commented as she continued with her work.

Surely, the photographer knew about her hair loss by now, but he didn't even bat an eyelash at her new hairdo. The wig she wore looked quite similar in color to her own hair, and it was a good fit. Once pack up was announced, she collected her belongings.

"Layla, wait a minute." The photographer came over. "Good job today. I believe we're working tomorrow with another client."

"Yes, we are." She couldn't quite meet his eyes. "I'll see you in the morning."

He rubbed his jaw. "I just wanted you to know I'm glad that you're continuing with your work despite—the troubles you're facing right now. This is true professional behavior, and I just wanted to congratulate you on it."

Amazed that he would show such support, she hugged him. "Thank you."

Feeling slightly better, she hailed a cab and went home. It was already eight in the evening. All she wanted to do was take a hot shower, have a meal, and go right to sleep. All this worrying about her hair and the continuous pressures of work made her feel tired. Entering her house, she felt surprised to find it dark.

Perhaps her mother didn't bother to come back.

With a sigh of relief, she strode in and dropped her keys in the bowl next to the main door. She pulled the wig off and shucked off the wig cap, thankful that Francis didn't use a lace-front wig, in which he might have had to use glue or tape, making it a little more complicated for her to take off.

A loud, piercing scream reverberated in the silence and Layla jumped. She ran back to the room and switched on the light. When the light flickered to life, she saw her mother, her arms wrapped tightly around her body, and rocking back and forth on the couch.

"Mom?"

"Go away."

"Mom—?"

"You—you—bastard." It seemed Mary could barely control her rasping breaths.

"Mom, what's going on?" Layla rushed over to her mother and stretched out her hand to comfort her.

Mary's eyes bulged. "Get away from me!"

Layla's stomach churned. She couldn't figure out what could have triggered this episode.

Mary slapped Layla's hand away from her shoulder. "Don't—don't hurt me." Mary was visibly trembling throughout her entire body. "Please don't..." Mary curled herself in the fetal position and clapped her hands over her ears.

Layla tried to understand her mother's rants. Mary's eyes were bloodshot and her disheveled appearance told Layla that she was drunk, but hallucinating? Or having a bad dream maybe?

"Oh, God—don't rape me—please—don't..."

When her mother continued to scream and yell while trying to push herself into a corner of the couch, Layla finally realized that her mother wasn't merely imagining stuff. She was reliving a horrific time of her life, the night she was raped in a dark alley on her way home from her job, then was left lying on the ground.

A month later, she discovered that she was pregnant and since she didn't believe in getting an abortion because of her strict Catholic upbringing, she had Layla and raised her on her own. But not without the trauma of being a victim of rape...not without silently resenting a rape-conceived child, reminding Layla on more than one occasion how she looked so much like her father, and nothing like her, except of course, for her hair.

While Layla never made light of her mother's experience that night, the life she knew growing up with the single parent, Mary, was extremely difficult. Yes, her mother was a victim, but she, Layla, became the forgotten victim.

Layla ran a hand over her barely-there hair. With this new haircut, she probably looked more like her father, the man who still preyed on Mary's peace of mind, even after all these years. "Mom, it's me."

Her mother continued to shriek in a loud voice. "Get away. Go away. Leave me alone!"

Seeing her so distressed, Layla didn't think there was any point talking to her. She ran to the door and picked up her keys from the bowl. After opening the door, she rushed out and banged the door shut.

Immediately, Mary's screams stopped.

Tears poured down Layla's cheeks as she realized that her mother linked her with the man who raped her. It'd been too overwhelming a thought for her to make peace with it. She'd lost her one and only connection with her mother—her hair that her mother prized.

Now, she didn't have anything in common with her own mother anymore. Layla realized she was trapped in a much bigger bind than she originally assumed and she didn't have any idea if she would ever get back to having a normal life again.

Chapter Four
The cost of not following your heart, is spending the rest of your life wishing you had. ~Amanda Helm

Clint Collins strolled into the hospital, feeling haggard and tired. He'd barely reached his apartment when he got an emergency call. Of course, he didn't have any option but to turn right back and attend to his patient. He loved his job and enjoyed interacting with young children while helping them get on with their lives. The sad part was Clint hated it when his patients lost their battle with death. "Are his parents here?" he asked the receptionist.

"No, Dr. Collins. They're on their way."

"I'll be in the room with him. When they come, send them straight in."

"Room 241, sir? Patient's name is Ethan Thomas, right?"

He sighed, ran a hand through his hair that probably already stood up in straight spikes, and nodded. Dread settled in his heart. "Yes, that's right."

Although he noticed the tall, svelte, yet voluptuous woman who stood with her back to him, he didn't pay her much attention as he strode towards his patient's room. He hated this part of his job.

Even after years of experience, he couldn't get used to this aspect of medicine. He wanted each of his patients to go home, healthy and happy. Pushing open the door, he walked inside and held the hand of the boy who was already in a deep coma.

Tears gathered in his eyes, but he hastily blinked them away. When the parents came in, he comforted them and stayed there until the Ethan stopped breathing. Clint noted the time of death in the chart. "I'm deeply sorry."

The mother was crying and incapable of speech.

The father put his hand on Clint's shoulder. "You did all you could, Doc. There were others who didn't even want to take a chance with him, but you tried your best. Ethan was very fond of you, and we had four beautiful years with him because of your hard work and persistence. We can't ever thank you enough for those."

Clint felt like a fraud and a loser. If he was so dammed good, he could have saved Ethan, but instead he failed him. He didn't have any words to express the grief he felt. He hugged Ethan's parents and left them to say goodbye to their son.

When he got out, he wiped a hand over his cheeks to brush away the last of his tears. Ethan was gone, but there were others who needed his attention. He felt optimistic that most of them were going to make it, but the ones who didn't—he never forgot them. His gaze strayed to the beautiful woman who was sitting on the bench against the door.

She looked very familiar, but there was something different about her hair.

"Hi. Do I know you?" When she stood up, he suddenly remembered. "Layla, right?"

"You have an excellent memory." She smiled a little hesitatingly. "I just came in to see if any of my test results were in, and then I heard about the boy—and I'm sorry, I couldn't help but follow you. Is he—is he...?"

Clint nodded. "He's gone." He could tell that she was deeply troubled about something. Surely, it couldn't be the death of his patient since she didn't know him, although he could tell that the news of Ethan's death disturbed her. Why was she here at this time?

Her gaze darted to the closed door. "I'm sorry. It must be hard to deal with the death of a young child."

"It is." Clint felt the urge to stay with her and talk, even though he didn't know her. Yes, he'd asked her out because she was beautiful and he'd been drawn to her, but there was also some other quality about her...her empathy. The way she'd talked to Charlotte and now, sadness she showed about Ethan's death told him she was highly sensitive.

He felt an immediate attraction to her. It wasn't just for her beauty, but also for her good heart which he could see easily. "Would you like to have a smoothie with me? There's a smoothie bar right outside. They serve coffee too, if that's what you prefer. I can't handle caffeine too well this time of the night."

She tilted her head. "Sure."

Amazed at his luck, he gestured with his hand.

She fell into step beside him.

"I'm sure you're wondering how I can ask you out at a time like this."

"You need to go on with a normal life, so you can help others." She adjusted the strap of her purse. "I appreciate the fact that you can deal with your grief and yet, continue to live."

He remembered that she was engaged. Or was that an excuse she gave, so she wouldn't have to say yes to his offer for dinner the other day? He didn't want to ask and spoil the moment. He also felt astounded at her keen perspective. "Are all your tests finished?"

"They might have to run a couple more of them." She sighed. "I'm losing my hair, and the doctors are trying to figure out why."

He didn't spare a glance at her wig. Naturally, she must be using it to hide the bald patches. Sympathy welled in his heart. She wasn't here to know about her test results at this time. Something else drew her here so late at night. He wasn't sure if he should ask her. "It must be very distressing for you."

"It was, until I overheard your conversation with the receptionist and then I realized that there were kids dying while I was moaning and groaning about my hair." She marched forward with an easy grace as they crossed the street. "It gave me a big jolt, and that's why I followed you."

He opened the door of the smoothie bar. Now, he understood her reasons. It wasn't often that people could put things in such perspective so early on. "Ethan was a very strong boy.

Although he wanted to live, he was a little tired of all the injections and treatment, but he didn't want to go, because it would make his parents distressed. But in the end, he lost. He left behind two younger brothers who have learned a lot from him about resilience and love. I'm sure he would be delighted to know that in some small way he could help you deal with your problems."

She slipped into the booth and put her purse on the side. "Thank you for saying that. You're a very kind."

He laughed. "That's not the impression I was trying to make."

Her eyes narrowed. "What impression did you want to make?"

"Cool. Competent. Charming. Those are the traits that I would have chosen to highlight."

Her lips lifted in a smile and she leaned back. "That too, doc, but what impresses me is that you can come back to see a patient when you're off duty. Most of us don't think that much about doing something for others." Her eyes brightened as if she had a sudden idea. "Is there a volunteer program at the hospital?"

"Yes, there is. Would you like me to give you some information about it?" Clint sensed in her a need to do something, and he wanted to encourage it. "Let me order first. What would you like? Coffee or a smoothie."

"I'll stick with a mango smoothie."

He ordered and got their drinks, Clint returned to his seat. After he gave her some information about the volunteer program at the hospital, he sat back to observe her.

He tried to recall any magazines on which he might have seen her or some billboards. His work kept him quite occupied and he barely got time to even watch TV. Also, he preferred to read or catch Broadway shows rather than sit in front of the idiot box. "I know you said you're a model but I...can't seem to recall any of your ads." Suddenly, something clicked in his memory. "Wait a minute. You're the IT girl, the cologne, right?"

Her lips lifted in a smile. "That was two years ago, but yes, I'm the IT girl."

"You're still doing their campaign?"

"Among others, yes." She sighed. "Now with this hair problem, I don't know how long I will continue to get work."

He understood her distress. It must be tough to deal with something that she didn't have any control over but might affect her work. If he were asked to leave his job, he wouldn't know what to do. "This isn't permanent, I'm sure of it."

"What if it's cancer or a tumor, or something like that?"

He sat back to observe her. "You look healthy to me. Your eyes are clear, and there are no obvious signs of fatigue. Have there been any changes in your skin?"

"No."

"Any fever? Bleeding? Trouble swallowing? Weight loss?"

She shook her head. "No."

"These are just basic questions, but based on that, I can say with a great amount of certainty that you don't have cancer. Have your test results come back?"

"A few did, and they are clear, but I'm waiting for more results."

He sipped his smoothie. Although he'd been tired before, being in her presence, Clint suddenly felt invigorated, energized. He didn't want the conversation to end. Somehow, he felt the need to talk to her. She needed him right now, and in a strange sort of way, he also wanted to spend more time with her.

"You must be thinking that I'm self-obsessed. I mean, after dealing with these sick children. Here I am boring you with my problems."

Clint leaned forward. He hoped that she could see the sincerity in his eyes. "You're worried, which is understandable. Anyone who faces such an issue would be anxious, but I want to assure you that it will get better. There's always a light at the end of the tunnel. More than hair loss, I think you must be more worried about the affect it might have on your job."

Much to his surprise, she wrinkled her brow. "Actually, I suppose, yes, I'm a little worried about that. Not that I love it...damn it. I shouldn't have said that. People assume that I love the glamour, but actually, it kind of loses its appeal after some time. I would rather do something else."

"What?"

She glanced out of the window and then looked back at him. "I don't know why I'm telling you this. I've actually never told this to anyone."

"Come on, you can share with me. I swear that I'm not affiliated with any news or media group."

She laughed. "I doubt it will make the headlines even if it was leaked, but I like to make soap."

He felt sure he misunderstood. "Soap?"

"Yeah, soap. In different colors and shapes, using organic products. I make it at home, but one day, I want to set up my own manufacturing plant that would make soap and sell it."

"Why don't you do it?"

"Time. Money. Effort. Everything is in short supply right now." Leaning forward, she sipped her smoothie. "It's not a big deal really. Maybe it's just a dream, you know. My career is doing great. It would be silly for me to leave it and pursue something so uncertain."

"Achievements are a direct result of pipe dreams."

"Who said that?"

He chuckled. "I did, just now," he admitted.

Her laughter filled the silence in the café. It was late, and there were no other customers around. He considered himself lucky that he got this opportunity to hang out with her. She was quite a lady. Open, honest, direct, and of course, mind-blowingly beautiful. It would be silly of him to let her slip through his fingers.

"Well said." She applauded and then checked her watch. "It's getting late. I should go home. Thank you for the smoothie and the talk. It was actually kind of nice."

"Kind of nice? Hmm...I was hoping to do better than that." He stood with her. Walking out with her, he surveyed the streets. No cabs were in sight. "Why don't we meet again and I could try to do a better job?"

"I don't know—it's...I'm in a difficult kind of a situation right now."

"You're engaged?"

When she looked away, he figured out that she didn't want to talk about it just as yet. If he pressured her, he might not get an opportunity to see her again. Clint held her hand and when she looked down at their linked fingers, he smiled. "Okay, we'll do it at your pace. Why don't you drop by the hospital to see me when you're there next?"

"I have to go now."

He let go of her hand. "Why don't I drop you? My car is in the parking lot, and it's late. I wouldn't feel comfortable letting you stand here while you tried to catch a cab."

Much to his delight, she nodded. "Thanks. That would be great."

Together, they strolled towards the parking lot. A nice, fast breeze blew through the street and he pulled the jacket tighter around his body. As far as Clint as concerned, this was a good start. Perhaps, in time, they would get to a better position but for now, he was happy to spend some time with her. .

He helped her into his car, and she gave him the address. Within forty-five minutes, he parked at the front of the building. Stepping out of the car, he jogged around his sedan to open her door. "This is a nice building."

"Actually, a friend of mine lives here. I'm going to stay here for the night.

"A friend?"

She stepped out of the vehicle, avoiding looking directly into his eyes. "Thanks for the ride. Take care."

"Bye." Clint watched her with her hips swaying enticingly, as she hustled to the front door of this friend's apartment, quite aware that she'd avoided answering his implied question. Friend? Was this her fiancé's place? He didn't think she was the kind of girl who moved from one man to another without much thought. Of course, there was nothing romantic about their relationship so far, but he hoped that eventually, it would move in that direction. But if she was still engaged, what was she doing alone in the hospital this time of the night? Why didn't she go to her own apartment?

So many questions swirled through his mind, but he didn't have any answers. After she stepped inside the building, Clint drove home. He could only hope that he would soon be able to get more answers. For now, it was enough that her lovely image floated in his mind, which was enough to sustain him for some time—or at least until they met again.

Chapter Five

Sometimes walking away has nothing to do with weakness, and everything to do with strength. We walk away not because we want others to realize our worth and value, but because we finally realize our own. ~Brigitte Nicole

Layla was on the set, as always, doing her work with quick aplomb. Although she didn't actually love her work, she enjoyed it because not only was she good at it, but also she'd put in many hours to perfect her craft. As she changed from pose to pose, her mind kept drifting to the delicious Dr. Collins...really a kind soul. She could read that about him. A doctor who went beyond his duty to care for patients; one who took out time to listen to the woes of a stranger, was certainly a man worth knowing.

"Take a break," Asher said.

Gratefully, she stepped off the set as they changed the backdrop. She walked into the changing room to change into a different outfit. Once she was done, she sat there to wait for them to call her back out.

Asher came in. "What happened last night, baby girl?"

All she'd told him was that she needed a place to crash. He didn't ask any questions as it was late at night and she didn't offer any information. "My mother wasn't—doing so well. She needed some space."

"She's living with you?"

There was no way she could share with anyone about what happened. It wasn't fair for her mother if she told her life story. Although, she trusted Asher, Layla wasn't prepared to tell him all this. "Just for a couple of days. Naturally, this problem that I'm facing...this hair loss is scaring the hell out of her. She seems to think that it's the end of my career."

"It might as well be," her manager, Bryan said, as he strode in. "You're different than other models because of your looks and your hair. It's not often a woman with black hair that has naturally blue highlights comes into the industry. If you can't boast this combination, there isn't much that you have to offer."

The shock of his statement hit her like a slap. The man was obnoxious.

As she bristled, ready to give him a scathing response, Asher jumped out of his seat. "You're the biggest moron that I've ever had the misfortunate to meet, man. Get the hell out!"

"You can't kick me out."

"Oh, yeah? Watch me do it" Asher strode forward and stood in front of Bryan. "I'll throw you out if I have to do it myself."

"Asher, leave him," Layla interjected. She didn't want a fight because of her. That would surely give the gossip columnists something to write about. She was lucky that so far, no one had mentioned her loss of hair, but this would certainly make matters worse. "Bryan, just go."

With a loud snort, he gazed into Asher's furious face, turned on his heels, and left.

Layla breathed a sigh of relief.

"The guy is nuts," Asher seethed. "Don't know why you put up with him."

Bryan was always a little over the edge but ever since she rejected his advances, he'd become even more so. Now, he was downright insulting. Maybe it was time to change her manager. Of course, it wasn't an easy choice. It would mean starting all over again with someone new, but if this kind of a behavior continued, she wouldn't have a choice.

Just one problem to add to my mountain of chaos!

Layla flopped back into her chair. "Let's just finish the work and go home."

Like a true professional, she didn't let her personal problems affect her work. Instead, Layla completed her shift and then bid goodbye to Asher.

"Are you coming to my place tonight?"

She nibbled at her bottom lip. Layla didn't have a clue about how her mother was doing. Even though the woman made her crazy, she needed to see if she was doing okay. "I don't know...I will let you know. Thanks for everything, Asher." She gave him a warm hug before striding off.

When she got out of the studio, her phone rang. She fished it out of her purse. It was Gage. She hadn't heard from him in a few days, but she assumed that he would take more time to decide on the future of their relationship. Perhaps he was already regretting his unkind words and wanted to apologize. "Hi," she said as she put the phone to her ear. Layla hoped to hear some good news. "How are you doing?"

"Layla, I've thought about our engagement and came to the conclusion that we're not the right fit for each other."

What the hell is he talking about? They were together for two years. How come he never thought about it before? "What?"

"It's just that...you don't get along with my parents, and that can't be good for our children, when we have them. And with your recent health problems...it's too much."

She was the one dealing with issues and yet, he was the one who complained of having too much on his plate. *Damn him to hell!* Layla fought the urge to bang the phone on the street. Good riddance! No way was she pleading with this guy. He didn't deserve to be in her life. "That's a good decision, Gage. I'm glad you thought about it. *Goodbye.*"

"Yeah—"

Layla cut the call and dropped the phone into her purse. A man who couldn't be there for her when she needed him wasn't worth her time. If he couldn't deal with issues that his parents had with her in all this while, she doubted that he would be able to resolve them after they were married. What the hell had she been thinking about when she agreed to marry him?

She must have been crazy to consider tying herself to this man for life. Even though she should've felt grief at the prospect of bidding goodbye to an old relationship that mattered so much to her not too long ago, now she only felt a sense of relief.

It's a good thing that he was out of her life. She didn't need him; she would deal with all her problems on her own, and she would be pretty damn good at it. More than devastation, she felt angered at the way he treated her. She hailed a crab. When she settled in it, her cellphone rang again.

If it were Gage, she wouldn't pick up. Instead, it was her mother. Uttering a long sigh, she picked up the phone. "Hi, mom. How are you doing?"

"Where the hell have you been? I'm dying from a massive headache. Had the most terrible nightmare...when are you coming home?"

Layla intended to go straight home to check on her mother, but hearing the petulant tone in her voice, she knew going in now would be a big mistake. Mary was seriously hung over. Her mother clearly didn't remember seeing her. It would better not to remind her about her haircut and her resemblance to her father until Mary was more in control. "I'm going to the hospital right now. Why don't you eat something? If you want I can order it for you."

"I just need some meds for this headache," groaned Mary. "I can't find any in your bathroom."

"They're in the kitchen cabinet, the one that's on the right hand side. I'll come in as soon as I can." After she hung up, Layla rubbed her forehead. "Excuse me, could you to take me to General Hospital, instead?" she told the cab driver.

Within a few minutes, she stood outside the hospital. Although her test results were not in yet, this seemed like a good time to take up the volunteering project that she talked to Clint about. Thinking about him sent a thrill of delight through her.

The man was pure pleasure. Perhaps it was odd for her to think about him just moments after she broke up with Gage, but the truth was that she never felt the instant connection with Gage that she now felt with Clint.

Still, she didn't plan to seek him out.

It might be a good idea to take some time to heal before getting into another relationship. It amazed her to realize that Clint didn't seem to care too much about her hair loss. He didn't just see her as a beautiful doll he could parade in front of people he knew, but rather as a person who was more than just a pretty face. After years of being treated like a trophy, it was nice to be thought of as a normal person.

When she registered at the reception as a volunteer, Layla felt a faint burst of joy in her heart. At last, she was now thinking beyond her own problems and concentrating on someone else.

"Which department would you like to volunteer in, ma'am?"

She thought about Charlotte, and yes course, she did want to see Clint again, but more than that, she wanted to be with kids who were so much stronger and more resilient than she was. "In the pediatric oncology department," she said.

She was given a badge and made to sign some forms. "You may go and show this to the nurse in charge. They'll assign you the days when you can come in and spend some time with the patients."

"Thank you." While she climbed the stairs, Layla wondered if Clint was on duty this time of the night. He probably had clinic hours as well and was busy with outpatients. When she reached the ward, Layla showed her card.

"It's nice to have fresh volunteers. Some of these children have been here for a long time, and it's wonderful if someone reads to them or plays with them. Which days are convenient for you, ma'am?" the nurse asked.

She chalked out a schedule. Once she was done, Layla didn't quite know what to do. She wasn't due to start until the next day, but she wanted to spend some time here. "Would it be okay if I met some of the kids?"

"Oh sure, ma'am. Please go ahead. You can't touch any of the equipment or medicines, but we do have an excellent collection of books here, and if you want, you can read to one of them."

Layla made her way inside the ward. The sight of pale, ill children brought tears to her eyes. What had she gotten herself into? Was she up to the task? Suddenly, she wasn't sure. What would she tell them? How would she introduce herself? As she stood rooted to the spot, pondering over her decision, her gaze was drawn to the girl on one of beds.

Charlotte?

She'd thought that the child was an outpatient. What was she doing here? Forgetting about her earlier doubts, she strode over to meet the girl. "Hi, sweetheart. How are you doing?"

The girl blinked her eyes. She looked pale and restless. "Layla? What are you doing here? Did you get sick?"

She resisted the desire to bite nervously at her bottom lip. "No, dear. I came here to visit you and the rest of the children. When did you come here?"

"Last night," she replied. "I wasn't feeling well, so the doctor decided that I should stay here for a few days. When I'm better, I can go home. Is your hair all better now?"

Seeing that Charlotte's mass of golden hair was half depleted, Layla didn't hesitate to take off her wig. "No, it's coming off a lot. I had to cut it."

"Did it help?"

She sighed. "Not really, but I'm sure it will get better if I eat right, and when the doctors give me medicines, I can start taking those as well."

"I don't think I'll ever get better." Tears pooled in Charlotte's eyes, and her lips trembled.

"You will," Layla assured her. She wanted to pick up the child and take her back to her home, but this was the best place for her to get treatment. "Do you want to play something with me?"

Charlotte's eyes brightened at the prospect. "Shall we pretend to be princesses? And when someone doesn't do what we want, we can tell them to write lines for the fairytale we are in."

"That sounds like a fun game." Picking up the extra blanket that lay on the child's bed, she tied it around her shoulders. "This shall be my dress, and I'm Princess Layla."

Charlotte giggled. She took off her blanket and draped it around shoulders. "I'm Princess Charlotte, and I can do magic."

Layla grinned, pleased that she was at least able to cheer up Charlotte a little. "Oh, can you? Show me."

It was sheer delight to play with the child. Charlotte had an active imagination and she could form a story and build around it. Forgetting her own woes, she concentrated on bringing a smile to the child's face. After about forty minutes, she sensed that Charlotte needed to rest. "Hey, sweetheart. Why don't we stop now, and I can come back tomorrow to play with you?"

Rather than protest, Charlotte lay down for a nap. She didn't seem to have much strength to continue. Bending a little, she dropped a kiss on the girl's forehead and strode out. It was enough for today.

Playing with Charlotte gave her more peace than anything else she'd done in ages. Her life was plagued by issues, but when she came here, she could forget everything else and help others who needed her.

As she said bye to the nurse, Layla heard Clint's voice from behind a screen.

He was talking to someone else. "I'm very concerned about the progress of some of my patients. Have you seen any signs of mold in any of the wards or treatment rooms?"

"No, doctor. I'm sure you're reading too much. It's normal…for us to lose patients."

"Not as many as these, Sarah, and not the ones I thought would pull through. I would like you to keep your eyes open for any sort of thing that might affect these patients. Perhaps some hygiene issues…I don't know. I'm grasping at straws here."

"I understand, doctor. We will all keep your concerns in mind."

She shouldn't have overheard the conversation, but now that she had, Layla didn't want to hide the fact that she knew something that was meant to be kept among hospital staff. She strode out to greet him. "Hey, Clint."

She'd assumed that he would be perturbed that she heard the conversation, but instead, he grinned. "Layla." He bent to kiss her cheek. "What are you doing here?"

"Volunteering," she said. They made their way out of the ward. "I saw Charlotte today. Wasn't expecting to see her, though."

"Yes, she hasn't been doing too well and I just wanted to keep her for a few days." He rubbed his jaw as he surveyed her. "I'm impressed with you though. It's not often that people who think about joining the volunteer program, actually do it. They talk about it, they debate it, and then they decide that they either don't have the time to keep it up or have other things that they need to finish. But you're here, and that's great."

"I'm serving my own interest too. It's nice to come here and see the kids." Layla glanced down, only to realize she was still holding the wig in her hand. Clint didn't seem to care. The way he viewed her was the same as when he saw her the first time or on the occasion after that. He didn't seem to care about her hair loss. It felt intoxicating to know that she could be viewed as a person, even with an almost bald head. "You seem more worried than when I saw you before."

He stopped in the middle of the corridor. "Guess you overheard that, huh? It's just—I have this feeling that I'm missing something important with some of my patients. Their treatment is right on track. They're being monitored, and the progress is good, and then suddenly...something happens and derails everything."

It couldn't be easy for him to live with tragedy on a regular basis. "Isn't that the way cancer operates?"

"No, actually it doesn't. Usually, I can tell the way it's going to roll, but these days, I'm stumped." He sighed and resumed walking. "I'll get to the bottom of this. In the meantime, I think we should stop meeting at the hospital. Would you like to have some dessert with me?"

Astounded at his direct question, she stared at him. Here she was, literally a bald girl with few prospects, but he didn't seem to care about that. "Dessert?"

"Sorry. I assumed you would have had dinner since it's late, but if you want, we could have dinner first. I've been thinking about these Belgian waffles all day. This guy sells them from a cart, and they're so good." He smirked. "Simply divine."

She laughed at his description. "Actually, I grabbed a quick sandwich before coming here, but I don't mind tasting these divine waffles."

"Let me just log out, and we'll be on our way."

"In the meantime, I'll use the washroom." She spared a rueful glance at her wig and hurried away.

On a date? With Clint? Layla couldn't believe it. Hours ago, she didn't have anything good happening in her life, and now suddenly, this guy made her feel as if she was someone worth spending time with, that she was important, and she mattered.

Layla swallowed the emotions that spiraled inside her. She really shouldn't read too much into his light offer. Perhaps he was only being sympathetic. Maybe this was his way of making her feel better about the whole mess that she was in.

The waffle cart was barely a block away from the hospital. The delicious aroma that wafted in lifted her spirits. "Smells great."

"Oh, you've got to taste them. I bet this guy is secretly an alien who is selling an aphrodisiac that has been secreted inside these waffles."

She laughed at his description. "And what is he trying to achieve by doing that?"

"Maybe the aliens are running an experiment on us."

"That sounds like a diabolical scheme. We really should be careful."

Clint signaled to the guy to give them two. "It might be better to eat as much as we can, so that others are spared."

She accepted the first plate.

He took his from the man and paid him. "Let's go sit over there." He pointed to a bench.

At this time of the night, not many people were around. Layla enjoyed the first bite when she was seated. The Nutella, strawberries, and whipped cream melted in her mouth along with the tender waffle. "Oh, my God!" She closed her eyes in rapture. "This is really divine."

"Told you, didn't I?"

Quietly, they sat and enjoyed the waffles. It was a beautiful night. A nice breeze blew and there weren't many cars on the road. Overhead, the curved moon shone, bright.

"So what's really bothering you?"

She didn't know what to say when he asked such a blunt question. "I'm losing my hair."

"It's not that bad. I mean, I know that to you, it seems like the end of the world, but really, it will get better. I don't think that's all that's on your mind, though."

Such a perceptive man. She didn't know him that well, but until now the people she loved and cared for were the ones who hurt her the most in some way or another. Perhaps she might find solace in the company of a person she didn't know that well. "I was dumped by my fiancé today. His excuse: his parents didn't like me because I'm a model, and of course, now that I'm bald, I probably lost all my appeal."

"I'm sorry to hear that, but frankly, I'm happy about this."

"Happy?"

"Sure. When you told me that you were engaged, my heart was broken, but now I'm feeling a little more hopeful about my chances."

She glanced at him. Was he flirting with her? Damn right he was. Amazed, as she was that he could still find her attractive after he'd seen the way she really looked, Layla was also a little scared. Is this a joke? Maybe she could meet this light tone. "If I got involved with you, it would probably be a rebound thing, you know that, right?"

"Ah! I don't think so." He shook his head. "I'm too awesome. Once you fall in love with me, you wouldn't want to let me go."

The laughter that sputtered out of her was genuine. The man was insane. "Love? We haven't even dated yet."

"And whose fault is that?" he demanded. "I've been asking you out for ages and you've been blowing me off. So how about dinner?"

"I must be crazy." She closed her eyes as if she wanted some holy intervention. "Okay, sure."

"Great." He pumped his hand in victory. "When and where?"

She didn't know what to say. Layla finished her waffle. Striding over to the bin, she threw in the paper plate. "How about we fix the time and date when we meet next?" It would give her time to ponder over this some more. "I should go now."

"I'll drop you. Same place as yesterday?"

"Actually no. That was my friend's house, as I told you. I'm going home tonight."

"And this friend of yours...he's not your fiancé, right?"

She raised an eyebrow. Was he feeling insecure? "I don't juggle men at the same time. Asher is a friend, and Gage, my ex-fiancé...is in my past."

"Good. So I'm the present. That's the way I like it." He smirked.

Layla wasn't sure what she'd gotten herself into, but as he dropped her home, her heart pounded with excitement. Clint seemed like such a delightful man, and she enjoyed spending time with him. Only time would tell as to how things would progress, but for now, she felt happy.

When he got out of the car and opened the door for her, she wasn't sure what he wanted to do. Her pulse picked up again, as she gazed into his eyes. He'd made his intentions pretty clear. Yet, she felt hesitant to take the next step forward. When his arms encircled her waist and he drew her forward, she didn't protest.

Oh, yes!

She wanted this.

His lips were soft on hers, and the kiss, was slow and passionate. All thoughts melted from her mind as she allowed herself to be carried on the hot current of desire that lanced through her veins. Sensations swam through her nerves and she enjoyed the way his lips moved over hers. When his tongue licked her bottom lip, she opened her mouth and allowed him to deepen the kiss. Layla was taken aback by the depth of her feelings. She never wanted this moment to end and yet, she was scared about what would happen if it didn't end.

When he finally stepped away, a wave of dizziness overtook her. The kiss, though too brief for her liking, was amazing.

He gazed into her eyes as if trying to figure out how she felt.

"I'll see you around," she managed to say.

Lifting her hand, he deposited a kiss on it. "Sooner than you think, Layla."

When he left, she staggered upstairs and into her apartment. Her life was irrevocably changed after that kiss. For better or worse, he'd become a part of it—and from now on, there was no looking back.

Chapter Six

If someone is not treating you with love and respect, it is a gift if they walk away from you. If that person doesn't walk away, you will surely endure many years of suffering with him or her. Walking away may hurt for a while, but your heart will eventually heal. Then you can choose what you really want. You will find that you don't need to trust others as much as you need to trust yourself to make the right choices.
~Don Miguel Ruiz

Two days after, Layla got the dreaded call from her doctor. Seeing his name flash on her phone screen, she felt a momentary jolt. Did he finally know what was wrong with her? "Hello, good morning."

"Layla, we have some news."

Good news? She didn't think so. "What is it?"

"Your test results have come in, and we've identified the reason why your hair is falling out. You've got alopecia.

Layla's heart thundered against her chest. "Alopecia?"

"Yes, it's an autoimmune disease in which your immune system attacks your hair follicles."

"Is it life-threatening?"

"Oh no, dear. Nothing like that. In most cases, the hair starts to grow back on its own within a year. However, in some cases, it doesn't come back. We would like to start you on treatments, though. I would like you to come in as soon as possible and we'll fix a regime for you."

She breathed a sigh of relief. It was a ray of hope. Once the diagnosis was made, and something was being done about it, she would feel a lot better. Helplessness had been the worst feeling. "Sure, I will."

"I'll ask my secretary to give you a call and set up an appointment."

"Thank you, doctor." She hung up. Despite feeling disappointed to know that she did have some kind of a disease, it was also reassuring to know there was a treatment for it. At least now, she had hope.

She felt a strong urge to investigate the causes of and treatment available for her condition. She switched on her laptop, logged on to Google and typed in the word alopecia in the search box.

She had every intention of being well-informed about the disease before her next doctor's visit. What she learned about alopecia stunned her. She was just one of tens of millions of American women who suffered from the disease every year.

Every year?

Unbelievable.

In addition, just as she'd first suspected, she believed that her inability to deal with stress could be one of the mitigating factors that led to her hair loss. After all, she wasn't on any medication, was in relatively good health and she couldn't have inherited the condition from her maternal relatives. Her father and his relatives were still a mystery to her, though.

She was relieved to see that there were a number of coping strategies available to hair loss sufferers, and she fully intended to try at least one of them, for now. She pulled in a deep breath and exhaled slowly. Tears welled up behind her eyes. This was one of the few times that she allowed herself to give vent to everything that'd been happening to her lately.

Suddenly, she felt lighthearted and better about what she'd been going through. And to be honest, it also helped that Clint didn't make her feel bad about her situation. By making her feel beautiful despite her problem, he burnt away the rejection she received from Gage and her own mother.

A sudden thought struck her. Were there any celebrities who suffered from alopecia? Layla leaned forward, as she typed in the question in the search box. She hit the enter button and waited for the results to load. She selected an article, with a click, and skimmed through it.

Wow! Quite a number of celebrities suffered from alopecia. Actress, Neve Campbell, cyclist Joanna Rowsell and fellow model, Naomi Campbell were just the few of them.

Feeling a lot more confident, she logged off, put her phone in her purse, and got ready for work. She silently vowed to do some more research about her condition when she got home. Of course, she would jot down those things that didn't seem to clear to her, so she could seek some clarification from her doctor.

After bidding goodbye to her mother, she went to the studio where she was supposed to shoot for a commercial. On the way to work, she took out her phone and sent a text message to Asher. "Starting treatment soon for hair loss. Will talk about it at work. See you soon."

There, now. She was moving forward already. Another woman might have been crushed to know she had some kind of disease, but Layla felt optimistic. Things would progress in the right direction. When she reached the studio, she pushed open the door and stepped through.

Not accustomed to seeing the place so dark, she blinked her eyes in confusion. Did she get the time wrong? Layla checked her watch. It was already eight in the morning. She was supposed to start makeup soon. The staff should have been here. Where were the studio employees?

Rather than waste her time, she hurried into the building and made her way to the back office. Abby, the studio manager, was probably inside. She would tell Layla what was going on. Maybe, they moved the shoot upstairs or something. Were they doing it on the roof? She stopped in midstride.

The man who stood in front of her was Bryan.

She put a hand on her heart. "You scared me. Thank God, you're here. Where is everyone else?"

"I don't know." Bryan's smile didn't quite reach his eyes. "In fact, I was about to call you. I heard that your engagement has been called off."

She winced. *Damn it! Had the news spread already?* She hated to answer so many questions. "Yes, it has."

"I'm sure you're hurting right now."

Her first thought was of Clint. He made her feel better. "Actually, I'm not." She shrugged. "It's a part of life. Don't worry about me, Bryan. I'm fine."

"Why don't we go and have lunch together and you can tell me all about it?" He gripped her arm. "Asher and his crew haven't come in. It's damn unprofessional of them, if you ask me. We should cancel today's shoot to teach them a lesson."

She tried to yank free from his grip. "Don't be silly. Something must have happened. Let me check with Asher." She made a move to get her phone from her handbag, but Bryan still hadn't released her arm.

His grip tightened. "I'll do it later. Why don't we go to my place first? I'm sure you want to talk more about this. Gage was never good enough for you." A sharp gleam showed in his eyes.

The nape of her neck tingled. A feeling of foreboding overwhelmed her. "I'm okay, Bryan." Her breaths quickened but she fought hard stay calm and to keep her voice firm, confident. "Leave me, alone."

"You're an attractive woman. Even if you lose every hair on your body, I would still be attracted to you." He pulled her as he marched towards the door. "Come on, let's go."

The faint fission of alarm was now a full blown avalanche of terror. "Bryan. What's wrong with you? Let me go."

"You're such a hard ass, Layla. Nothing is ever good enough for you." When he yanked her hard, she nearly fell over.

Layla screamed but he pinned a hand on her mouth and yanked her against his body. The thump of her heartbeat thrashed loudly in her ears and her blood grew cold. What did he plan to do? Was he going to force himself on her?

While she kicked and groaned, he dragged her into Abby's room. Throwing her on the couch, he closed the door. "Now, you can't get away."

"What are you doing?"

"I should've done this a long time ago. Women like you don't understand pretty words. You want a man to show you how it should be done."

Was he actually planning to rape her? Had he gone mad? She lunged for the door.

He grabbed her waist and threw her on the couch once more.

"Have you lost your mind?"

"Yes, I have. And you will too, when you see what I've got to show you." He fiddled with the buttons of his shirt and shucked it off. "You're going to have a great time, baby."

She dug into her purse to get out the pepper spray but as soon as she pulled it out, he snatched it out of her hands. Layla wished she'd taken the time to learn self-defense. If she got out of this, it would be the first class she enrolled into. "I don't want this, Bryan. Let me go right now."

He leered at her. "I know what you *really* want."

Layla screamed and screamed. She darted to the side and tried to pick up a chair, but it was too heavy. He'd lost his mind. If she didn't do something, he would definitely rape her. Was she destined to end up like her mother? She couldn't bear the atrocity of it. This wasn't fair.

She'd trusted this man, and he betrayed her in the worst possible way. Picking up the paperweight from Abby's desk, she threw it at him but he dodged. It shattered against the wall. Layla ran towards the door, but he rammed into her with enough force to make her dizzy. She fell on the tiled floor and he leaned on top of her.

Grabbing her arms, he pinned her hard.

She kicked him in the groin.

With a groan, he let her go.

Heaving him off, she tried to make her way towards the door but he grabbed her hand. He stood and pushed her. She fell against the desk. Her thigh hit the table so hard that a scream of pain gushed from her lips. He fell on top of her. She was now pinned between his body and the desk. With one hand, he grabbed her wrist and with the other, he tried to yank off his trousers.

She hit him repeatedly on the head with her free hand. Layla tugged his hair hard enough to make his head shake but he refused to get off. She scratched his neck with her nails. Again and again, she screamed. Was this how it would end? Was he going to get his way with her? Could she do nothing to stop him?

Suddenly, his weight was dragged off her and he fell on the floor. "You bastard!" Asher shouted. Picking up the heavy chair, he held it over Bryan. "I'm going to kill you."

"No, Asher, please. Don't waste your time and energy on this fool." She didn't want her friend to go to jail for assaulting the guy. "Leave him." Relief flooded through her when she realized she'd been saved just in time. If Asher didn't come, this man would have violated her body. Layla kicked him while he lay cowering on the floor.

Asher lowered the chair. Putting his arm around Layla, he led her to the door. "I'm going to call the police."

She picked up her purse. Her mother never reported the rape because she was scared of humiliation, but Layla was made of sterner stuff. "Let's get out and do it. I can't stand to see him."

Outside, she dialed 911 and made her complaint. Asher put a chair under the door handle, so that Bryan couldn't open it. "I got your message and was surprised that you didn't know that the studio was closed for an emergency renovation of their fire alarm system. We canceled the shoot and informed Bryan. He was supposed to tell you."

"He must have realized that it was the perfect opportunity to get me alone." Layla shook her head as she pondered over the man's diabolic nature. Did he really think that if he forced himself on her, she would remain quiet? Perhaps other women wouldn't say anything and let bygones be bygones, but she didn't want to give him another opportunity to do the same to someone else. If she didn't hold him accountable, he would be free to do the same to someone who didn't know about his true nature.

"When I got your message, I thought something must be wrong, since you didn't know about the cancellation and rushed here to find out what was going on."

She didn't even want to think about what would have happened if he hadn't turned up. "Thank you."

When the police came, it took a lot of time and effort. Luckily, the evidence was right on hand. They bagged the skin that came out from under her fingernails. Bryan's body was inspected for injury marks that she left on him.

Asher gave his statement. It was a long process. The police offered to take her to the hospital, but she declined. More than her body, her spirit was hurt by Bryan's actions. He was responsible for shaping her career. For years, she trusted him, and this is how he repaid her.

Once the formalities were all over and Bryan was taken to the police station, Asher offered to drop her home.

"I need to go to the hospital."

"Why? Is everything okay?"

"I volunteer at the pediatric wing." Layla felt the urge to be with the kids who needed her.

Asher dropped her off and she went inside. Charlotte was still in the ward. Layla spent her time playing with her. Later, she read to all the children. It was the best part of her day.

"Can we pretend to be princesses again?" demanded Charlotte.

"Sure, sweetheart."

"Why don't you be a princess, and I'll be evil monster who locks you in a tower?"

Layla laughed at the girl's description. The child sure had a creative imagination. "Alright, I'll do it, but there's no tower here."

"We'll pretend that the closet is the tower."

"Closet?"

Charlotte pointed to a door that was opposite the nurse's desk. "That closet. They keep supplies there."

"I don't think the nurse will like that."

"We can ask her," she said.

Layla held her hand. "Okay, let's ask her." Together, they marched to the nurse's desk. Much to her surprise, Clint stood there. "We've got to stop meeting like this," she joked.

"Layla!" He kissed her on the cheek. "Hello, Charlotte." He patted the child's head. "Ready to go home? Your mom is coming to pick you up."

Charlotte sighed as if that was the worst news she'd ever heard. "Do I have to? I like it here. Layla comes here and I won't get to see her when I go home."

Feeling touched, Layla bent to hug the girl. "I'll ask your mom if I can come visit you."

"But we were going to play princess, and I wanted to lock you in the closet."

"What?" Clint stared at them, bemused. "Which closet?"

Layla explained the rules of their little game. "She wanted to find out if she can lock me in that tower." She pointed at the closet.

Clint stared at the door. Striding over, he held it open. "I don't think there's much space here and her mother must already be on her way."

When he gazed into the closet, she saw an odd look on his face.

He marched inside.

Feeling a little surprised by his abrupt manner, she clutched the girl's hand and led her back to the bed. "Listen, sweetheart, your mom will be here soon. Why don't we play when I come to your house?" She convinced the girl to pack her belongings and wait for her mother while she went back to the desk. Layla opened the closet door.

Clint was inspecting a tube.

"What's wrong?"

"These contain the old pieces that come from the machine at the treatment room."

"But?"

He shook his head. "They're supposed to be discarded properly and not strewn about in this haphazard manner."

She didn't know what to say, she still felt baffled by his behavior.

Putting down the tube, he strode out. "Let's go."

She followed him out of the ward. "What's going on, Clint?"

"I'm just trying to figure out if everything is in order. There has to be another reason why my treatments are failing."

Layla drew in a deep breath. "I've got to tell you something." Now that he was a part of her life, she needed to update him. Layla definitely didn't want him to find out things from the newspaper. She hoped that it didn't come to that, as she didn't want the gossip, but at the very least, she should inform him beforehand. Layla told him about Bryan's attack.

He clasped her hand after hearing the tale. "Are you all right? You should've called me."

"Asher was there and he helped me. Everything is fine, but I will have to look for a new manager now."

He kissed her hand. "You're a brave woman, Layla. Is there anything I can do for you?"

"No, thank you." She felt touched by his concern. "I'm just going home now."

"Can I drop you?"

"Okay, thanks."

Together, they left the hospital. When she sat in his car, Layla felt safe, happy. She could see that he was still upset by the deaths of his patients and was conducting his own investigation.

When he parked in front her apartment building, he got out and opened her door. "Layla, we should go out soon. How about dinner tomorrow?"

She'd promised him that they would and frankly, she was ready. "Sure. Pick me up at seven."

The kiss caught her by surprise. Desire, wild and strong, careened through her system and slammed into her heart. She wanted more. This wasn't enough. Her arms snaked around his neck and she held on while her body melted against his. It felt great to be held by a man who cared. Yes, she still felt self-conscious about her hair loss, but now she felt like a woman again.

When they separated, she touched his lips. Although she longed to ask him to join her for light snack, her mother was still at home and she definitely didn't want to answer her questions about Clint.

"See you tomorrow, Layla."

With reluctance, she stepped away and went upstairs. Now, there was so much more to look forward to. Her treatment was about to start, and she had a new friend, one who was worth her time and effort.

Chapter Seven

*Fall in love with someone who falls in love with your flaws
and thinks you're perfect just the way you are.* ~Brigitte Nicole

When Clint rang the bell, Layla was ready. She checked her reflection in the mirror one last time and literally skipped over to open the door. She wore a Persian red, smocked tube-top maxi dress. Her size nine feet were encased in a pair of open-toe, wedge sandals, complete with an ankle buckle closure. He daintily polished toenails, were painted in beige, a neutral shade, which accentuated the color block sandals, which were of various shades of red and white. "Hi."

"Wow! You look amazing." Clint leaned over to kiss her on the cheek. He handed over the white tulips he held in his hands. "For you."

"Aww! How sweet. Come in."

Clint walked in and surveyed the place. "Nice apartment." He pointed to the picture hanging on the eastern wall. "Is that a Leonardo print?"

"Yes, it is. Can't afford the real thing, so it's a good thing to look at when I feel down."

"Yeah, I'm a huge fan of his." He turned when he heard the tip-tap of Mary's heels.

"Hello."

Taking out the vase from a cabinet, Layla filled it with water. "Clint, this is my mom, Mary Turner. And mom, this is Dr. Collins."

"Pleased to meet you, Ms. Tuner."

Mary pressed her lips together in a fine line. Layla had already told her about her break up with Gage, but she didn't seem very happy to see that her daughter had already moved on. She sniffed. "You're a doctor?"

"Clint works in the General Hospital in the Pediatric Oncology department. He's a specialist."

Mary frowned as she watched her daughter put the flowers in the vase. "Layla, I've decided to shift back home. You're obviously doing well now."

"No problem, mom." Strolling over, she hugged her mother. She would never tell her mother how badly upset she'd been that night when Mary mistook her for Layla's father. "Thank you for coming to stay with me. I'll come back early enough to help you pack."

"I've already done it." Mary ran her hand over the countertop. "I'm going to leave after you."

"Okay mom. Take care."

After bidding goodbye to her mother, Layla left with Clint.

"I didn't know your mother was staying with you," he said.

Layla was glad things were working out fine. Mary was a disturbing element in her life, but she did love her mother and wanted them to have a good, solid relationship. By not confronting her about that incident, she actually did a lot of good. Perhaps on some level, Mary realized the harm she'd caused her daughter and didn't want to do it again. "She was here for a few days," Layla finally said with a dismissive wave of her hand. "So, where are we going?"

"I've got booking at the Plaza."

"Ahhh...Nice choice. I love their food."

He smiled. "Good then, I'll cancel the alternate booking at Bellagio. Unless, you prefer to go there."

She laughed at his enthusiastic response. He really seemed to be keen on making her happy. It was such a change from her past relationship that she didn't quite know how to respond to it. "The Plaza, I think."

As they drove to the restaurant, they made small talk. It just seemed so easy to talk to Clint. He was knowledgeable about many topics. She liked the way he could switch from subject to subject without a pause. She'd thought doctors were driven and focused while lacking time to read much, but he acted quite well aware of things that went on in the world. She appreciated this as another great quality about him.

Once they were seated in the restaurant, he ordered quickly after consulting with her.

"So, how are things in the hospital? Have you found out anything that's causing problems with your treatment?"

He frowned. "I'm working on it. Actually, I think I may be close. Let's keep our fingers crossed that I can deal with the problem before I lose another patient."

She held his hand. "I'm sure you will. Clint, I can't tell you how happy it makes me to see you so dedicated to your patients."

He glanced down at their linked fingers. "Takes one to know one. Layla, I'm impressed with your courage."

She let go of his hand, feeling a little embarrassed by her direct words and actions. It astounded her to realize she actually felt comfortable enough with him to say all these things without thinking ten times about them. "Look at us talk. We sound like a mutual admiration society."

"That's a healthy start for a relationship."

A relationship? Since when did they jump from a date to a relationship? Her heart thundered in her chest as she realized that it felt so right the way he said it. She should've been devastated by her break-up with Gage, but instead Layla considered it the best thing to happen in her life. It led her to Clint, and also it saved her from making the worst mistake possible. "So, what's your favorite place in New York?"

"Hmmm! That's a question that could take days to answer." He smiled. "As a die-hard New Yorker, I have to say that I love everything about this city, but of course, Central Park is the one place that always brings a smile to my face."

"I like going there too," she admitted. "Another favorite haunt of mine is the—Hudson River."

"—Hudson River," he said at the same time.

Together, they burst out laughing. "I guess we like a some of the same things."

For a few, intense seconds, their gaze clashed, until Layla looked away.

Clint cleared his throat, which served to break the brief moment of awareness. He reached for his glass. "It's a pity you're not a doctor. I bet you would have been good at it." He took a sip of water.

"I never considered medicine as a career." Layla chuckled. "Too much studying and frankly, I got into modeling relatively easy when I compare it with how difficult others have had it." She mimicked his gesture and took a sip of her water. "My mother sent my pictures for a contest when I was twelve. I got selected and started getting small jobs, and then finally, I got a major break." She smiled. "For now, it's enough that after years of online studies, I eventually completed my bachelors in business management."

He gazed at her for a long moment with a smile on his lips

When the waiter brought their appetizers, they both dug in.

"Um, I shouldn't ask...it's none of my business...but I sensed some awkwardness between you and your mother."

Sometimes, Layla felt as if he could delve in her heart and read the emotions. "You're right." She took in a deep breath. For too long, she'd suppressed her feelings regarding her mother, focusing instead on her work. She never felt comfortable telling Gage everything even though they were a couple for so long, but somehow it was easy to tell Clint. She told him about her mother's state of mind, her past, and the connection she made between Layla and her father the other night.

"So that's why you were in the hospital? You wanted to avoid going home?"

"Yeah, something like that, and I'm glad that I met you that night."

Across the table, he held her hand. "Your mother's demons don't have anything to do with you. You're nothing like your father who deserved to be thrown in jail for what he did, but his crime has no bearing on your personality...or your life. Your life is your own, and you should live it the way you want. And as far as your hair is concerned, let me tell you that with or without it, you're beautiful."

His gaze flitting across her every feature, felt like brief, loving touches.

"Your eyebrows are beautifully arched, and I can tell you didn't have to tweeze or wax them to hell and back to get them that way." His fingers glided softly across each eyebrow. "And your lips, Layla...they tempt me every time I look at you." He smiled in response to her gasp of surprise. "Like now, I want to kiss them, but I won't. At least not now...not yet."

She could feel the warmth of his fingers seeping in her hand, traveling across her veins, straight inside her heart. No man made her feel as if she was special in quite this way before. "Thank you. It means a lot to hear you say that."

He let go and they resumed eating. Instead of continuing the conversation, he switched to another topic. Probably he realized that she wouldn't be able to talk more about it. "So what about your soap manufacturing plan?"

She laughed out loud. "I can't believe you remember that. That was just talk. I don't think I would ever be able to do it. I'd thought that I would get into a lot of trouble when people began to know that my hair was falling out, but much to my surprise, I have gotten a lot of support from odd corners. Photographers, makeup artists, and even some models have come up to me and told me that I shouldn't worry about this."

"There are a lot of good people in the world."

"You're right, and you're one of them."

"Now, you're trying to flatter me."

She gave him a winning smile. "You're probably right."

He rolled his eyes and they both laughed.

As they continued to talk, she was amazed that nothing seemed to faze him. For a long time they talked, laughed, and ate. When the dinner came to an end, she was actually sorry about it because they were having such a good time.

"Would you like to come to my house to see Mr. Rufus?"

She tapped her foot on the pavement as she eyed him. Was this an excuse for him to get her inside his apartment? "Mr. Rufus?" She shook her head. "I have heard some good lines before but that one is just..." She laughed. "...Strange as all hell."

His eyes rounded as he got her joke and he chuckled. "My cat! Unless he approves of you, I don't think I'll be able to go out with you again."

More laughter sputtered out of her lips. "Why? Is he your dating consultant?"

"Yep! And he's very strict. He has definite ideas about the kind of woman that I should date, and if he doesn't like you, we may as well call it quits right now."

She stared into his eyes. The storm of emotions that coiled in their depths startled her. She could sense he liked her a lot. Sure, their chemistry was off the charts but did she want to get involved with a man so soon after a breakup?

She really should say no. They shouldn't do this. "Yes," she said even before she realized that she intended to acquiesce. *Damn it! He must be a wizard.* Slowly, he was casting a spell on her that was proving harder and harder to break. But did she really want to escape his web? Layla wasn't sure.

The only thing she felt confident about was that she didn't want to let go of this opportunity. She wanted him with a desperation that shocked her. It was getting harder to fight her attraction to the good doctor, and suddenly she didn't want to do it anymore. Walking over to his car, she waited for him to open the door. She settled in.

Now, Clint drove the car with an intense concentration.

Silence reigned. There were no more words between them. The need was too great, and it could only be expressed in one way.

When they reached his apartment, he parked the car and led her upstairs. The two flights up to his apartment seemed to take forever.

As soon as they stepped inside, and he closed the door, he drew her in his arms. Yanking her body hard against his, he pressed his hard muscles against her soft curves. His lips found hers, and she opened her mouth to accept his tongue. His hands roamed over her body, as their lips remained fused.

The kiss was hot and fiery.

She could feel the passion that spiraled in his veins. It matched hers. She didn't want to wait anymore.

He lifted her full-figured frame almost effortlessly.

It really took a real man who could handle a woman of any size, she joked silently.

Clint took her to his bedroom.

All she saw was a mahogany, four poster bed, two matching chairs, and a large TV on the wall before he laid her down. Their clothes came off in a flurry of movements.

Layla raised her hand to her wig, hesitant, uncertain. What would he think about her bald head? She still had some stubble, but without the wig, he might think she was ugly. As if all the sweet, yet seemingly earnest words he'd whispered to her at the Plaza, had been forgotten, she paused.

As if understanding the fear that coursed through her veins, he bent over her. "Layla, you're beautiful, alluring. I think of you like that and there is no way, no how, anyone or anything can change it."

She still couldn't muster the courage to take her wig off. Not now. Layla left it on.

He nodded his head as if he understood the internal struggle she wrestled with.

On the one hand, she wanted to believe his words, but on the other, it was still a bit difficult to shake off the way Gage had made her feel...so small, so insignificant, so ugly, when he found out about her condition.

Clint didn't say anything, instead, his lips found hers.

When she nipped his bottom lip in between her teeth, he let out a groan.

His hands found her breasts and squeezed.

The desire that undulated inside her was strong and healthy.

Trailing a line of kisses down her throat, he took one nipple in his mouth.

Her body arched as a current of pleasure zipped through her veins. Her hands skidded over his smooth, lean back as she enjoyed the way his muscles rippled under the tips of her fingers.

Flicking his tongue over her nipples, he gave them new life. Slowly and gently, he caressed each hard bud until they were swollen and aching with need.

She wriggled under him, breathless with desire.

His erection pushed against her taut stomach. Burying his face in between her breasts, he inhaled deeply, as if trying to revel in the fragrance that emanated from her body. His mouth moved over her breasts, fondling and caressing them.

She loved it.

Layla ran a hand down his body until she found his hard, long length. When it twitched between her fingers, she felt her own passion turn into a storm.

In response, his hand slipped down until he reached the curls that guarded her moist centre. His finger slid into her warmth. Rhythmically, he moved his finger in and out and she bucked under him.

An orgasm ripped through her body, careening inside her like a storm that she had no control over.

Removing his finger, he took the opportunity to reach for the foil package on the bedside table, ripped it open with his teeth, and slipped on the latex protection, while Layla took big, shuddering gulps of air. Slipping up along her torso, he licked the beads of sweat that lined her breasts. When she was still and silent, he parted her legs and took position. He slid inside her as if he were slicing through molten butter.

Layla didn't think she would be ready so soon, but her muscles expanded to accommodate him. The passion and need that glided through her nerves was a huge surprise. She was so ready to do this.

The ride started once more, and the pace he set was brutal. He pounded into her, hard. Fast. Her fingers clutched his hips as he slid in and out. Her nails dug into his skin, urging him to go faster. His chest brushed over her breasts and her nipples ached. His cologne, hot and spicy, hit her nostrils and invoked a desire that she thought wasn't possible.

The momentum carried her higher and higher until she was a mass of quivering, shuddering muscles. The craving for release was so strong that she felt like her body was on fire.

She felt him join her on the apex of the cliff that beckoned her forward. With each thrust, she felt freer, lighter, until she was swaying right at the cusp. Layla screamed as the second orgasm ripped through her, turning her insides into jelly. Her toes curled and she shuddered. A moment later, he spilled his seed inside the barrier and collapsed on top of her.

For a long time, they lay still, each lost in thought. Never before did a man make her feel quite this way. She simply didn't have the energy to move out from under him. He rolled off her and still she couldn't move.

This wasn't just the release of the sexual tension that gripped her since she saw him. This was love—and suddenly—Layla felt scared. If he could make her feel like this in one night, what else lay waiting in the days, months, years to come? It was the last thought on her mind as she drifted into sleep beside him.

It was the beginning—and she couldn't wait for the rest of the journey to unfold.

Chapter Eight

You don't need anyone's affection or approval in order to be good enough. When someone rejects or abandons or judges you, it isn't actually about you. It's about them and their own insecurities, limitations, and needs, and you don't have to internalize that. You're allowed to voice your thoughts and feelings. You're allowed to assert your needs and take up space. And you're allowed to remove anyone from your life who makes you feel otherwise. ~Daniell Koepke

Clint was in the midst of a nice dream when he heard the shrill sound of his phone. Rolling over, he grabbed it and saw the name on the screen. *Shit! It's the hospital administrator.*

He picked up the phone. "Hello, Mark. What is it?"

"Clint, what is this that I'm hearing about the investigation that you're carrying out on the deaths that have taken place in your department?"

Clint sat up. His gaze took in Layla who was still in deep sleep. Rolling out of the bed, he strolled out of the room with the phone tucked between his ear and shoulder, so as not to disturb her. He checked the time. It was eight in the morning. Since it was Saturday, he wasn't expected to be in the hospital. "It's not an investigation. I'm only trying to see if there's some sort of negligence going on that is the cause of so many unexpected deaths."

"Negligence?" Mark yelled. "Have you lost your mind? A word like that is taboo in our hospital. Do you know what could happen if the media got wind of your so-called investigation? And what if the parents get to hear about it?"

Clint rubbed his forehead. Sure, he hadn't considered the possible ramifications if his hunch was right, but he couldn't wash away the doubts that plagued his mind. "Four children are dead. They could've lived—at least, that's what I thought."

"Cancer doesn't move in expected ways. It's possible that you're clutching at straws just because you don't want to accept the final outcome."

Clint huffed in annoyance. Everyone was telling him the same thing. Sure, it was a possibility but Clint had been working with kids for a long time. He knew the way these things worked. Some patients died despite his best efforts. That was expected. But these four…he wasn't so sure. Something was seriously amiss in his calculations or else there was another factor at play that no one else was willing to consider. "You could be right."

"I. Am. Right," Mark insisted. "You're stirring up trouble, Clint. And I can't accept it. Come in now and we'll talk."

Shit! Clint didn't like it. Sure, he could be way off the mark but his instincts told him that he wasn't wrong. Something was amiss with the way the children were being looked after. He'd double checked the treatments that were given and the lists of medicines that he prescribed. Nothing was out of order—and yet he couldn't let it go. "Okay. I'll come in."

"Now. I'm waiting," Mark barked before he cut the call.

Clint rubbed his eyes as he put the phone on the table. What the hell was going on here? Could he be wrong about this? He wasn't so sure. In fact, he was quite positive that he was on the right track. All he needed was one clue, but somehow he wasn't getting it.

"What's wrong?"

He whirled around

Layla stood at the bedroom door.

"Sorry. Did I wake you up?"

She nibbled her lips. Uncertainly swirled in her eyes. All she wore was his t-shirt that he'd discarded last night.

Even with her eyes heavy with sleep and no makeup, she was the most beautiful woman he'd ever seen. Strolling over, he drew her in his arms.

"I've got to go," she said.

He sighed. Clint wanted to take his time to have breakfast with her. Perhaps they could have gone to a nearby bakery and shared a croissant and coffee. He longed to do all the normal things that people did when they had time and wanted to spend it with each other, but of course, he had things to do. He couldn't ignore Mark's summons. "I've got to go, too. The hospital administrator wants to see me."

Layla's eyes widened. "Did you lose another patient?"

"No. We just need to talk about some measures that I've been taking." Regret flooded through his heart. He wanted nothing more than to be here with her, but of course, it wasn't possible. He lifted her chin with his finger and pressed his lips against hers. For a few moments, he felt as if she held back, but then her mouth opened and his tongue delved in. It was heady to taste her mouth once more, to explore the hidden depths, and the nooks and crannies that excited him. Finally, he released her and stepped away. "I don't want you to go."

She smiled. "Okay, then let's stay in."

He pulled a face. "It's work. Damn it! How about I pick you up afterwards? Or better still, why don't you stay right here and I'll come back as soon as I can."

She cocked her head. "I've got to go home, take a shower, and change. How about I meet you afterwards at the smoothie shop across from the hospital?"

"Yeah, that sounds like a plan. Give me a couple of hours. I'll call you when I'm done. Now that I'm going in, I might as well check on my patients too."

"They're lucky to have you as their doctor."

"And I'm lucky to have you." He dropped a kiss on her lips and took a moment to run his hands over her voluptuous hips. Man! She was solid. It was crazy the way desire triggered in his gut every time he looked at her. With an effort, Clint pulled away. "See you soon."

After a quick shower and a hurried breakfast, he dropped her at her apartment and drove to the hospital. As expected, the meeting with the administrator didn't go well. The man all but accused him of creating trouble and putting the hospital's reputation at risk. Clint could understand the reason for the man's dismay. If news regarding this leaked out, they might get sued. It wasn't a pleasant scenario but neither was death.

Clint stood his ground. "I will agree to not making my concerns public, but that's all I am willing to concede. If there's something wrong with the way we're treating the patients or if there's indeed some negligence, we need to take a look at it before someone else discovers anything about it. I'm not going to be involved in any sort of cover up."

"There's no cover up. If you had a shred of evidence to support your theory, I would back you one-hundred percent, but until then, I command you to keep your mouth shut."

Clint pursued his lips in a thin line. He didn't like the way the man talked to him. If Mark was trying to intimidate him, he wasn't doing a good job. He wasn't willing to back down at any cost. "Command?"

"Yes, command. I know that you enjoy a stellar reputation, but you also need goodwill to survive, and if you pull stunts like this, it might be harder for you to remain here at General Hospital."

"Are you threatening to fire me?"

"I'm not threatening, but telling you the truth. Now, please...I urge you to reconsider this false trail and concentrate on the job that you do so well."

"What—"

"Goodbye."

Clint hated to be dismissed in that cursory manner, but he knew that there wasn't much he could do to convince Mark. Yes, he didn't have proof. Yes, he wasn't sure as to what was wrong, but there was something serious going on in his department and he was determined to get to the bottom of this mystery. He strode out and went straight to the pediatric oncology ward.

Even though he wasn't on duty, he took some time to talk to his patients and then called Layla. She didn't pick up so he left her a text. After about thirty minutes, he walked out and strolled into the smoothie shop. She wasn't there yet so he sat to wait.

Ten minutes later, she came in.

Like always, the sight of her reduced the anxiety that bubbled in his heart.

"What's wrong?"

Shit! He didn't want to burden her with his troubles. "Nothing much. Just got a rap on my knuckles for saying stuff."

She sat opposite her. "I hope it's nothing serious."

"Don't worry about it."

After he ordered, Clint tried to relax. There wasn't much that he could do right now, so he might as well enjoy his time with Layla. They talked, and it was such a glorious, wonderful morning that they ended up staying at the smoothie bar far longer than he planned. Finally, Clint pushed aside his glass. "Ready?" He honestly felt reluctant to separate from her. "Why don't we go for a walk and then have lunch?"

She fiddled with her head wrap in a seemingly unconscious gesture. "Clint, where is this going?"

His heart thundered in his chest. Now that she asked him out loud, he felt hesitant to spill out whatever was in his heart. What if she didn't like his answer? What if she was scared away by his reply? "I like you, I suppose that much is obvious...but I think what may not be obvious is that I'm falling in love with you. Fast."

Her eyes widened in surprise.

"I suppose it's crazy to think in those terms when we've barely dated."

"Barely," she whispered out the words. "I mean—we don't even know each other."

"Our hearts recognize each other," he said. Clint meant every word. Ever since he met Layla, he'd known with an absolute certainty that there was something special about this woman. She was THE ONE. Sure, he backed off pretty quickly when she told him that she was engaged but now that she was with him, he didn't want to waste time playing games. Together, they were cool. Together, they were good.

And he wanted to keep this spark alive.

She shook her head.

Fear coursed through his veins. Did she regret that they'd made love? Was she going to get up and walk? Had she been taken aback by his frank admission?

Instead, she leaned back and studied him. "Clint, I have to admit that I feel the same way."

Delight was a like a drug inside him. "You do?"

"I suppose it's crazy—but it is what it is."

He leaned forward and held her hand. "Wow! I feel like I'm on top of the world."

The sound of her of her bubbly laughter was like music to his ears. He wanted to see her this happy and carefree all her life. "Same here. Come on now, let's get out of here."

When he slid out of the booth, Clint was taken aback when he saw his much married colleague walk in with a woman who was definitely not his wife. He worked closely with Warner. The man was responsible for maintaining and operating the linear accelerator that dispensed radiation to the children who came in for cancer treatments.

This was definitely not Warner's day off. Clint slipped out of the booth and marched over to the man as he stood at the counter, holding hands with the woman. "Hey."

The flush of color and the shifty glance that Warner gave him told Clint that Warner wasn't supposed to be here. Or perhaps he was just wary of being caught with someone other than his wife.

"How is it going, Clint?"

"Good. And you?"

"I'm all right." He began to turn away, clearly not willing to talk. "See you."

"Aren't you supposed to be on duty right now?"

"Just slipped out for a break."

"But I checked in the ward and you're due to give three treatments today."

"Yes, and I'll do them all. Now, if you will excuse me..." He turned his back on Clint.

Clint frowned. This could be nothing, or else perhaps this was the first validation he got that something wasn't right with his ward. Rather than question the man further, he clasped Layla's hand and walked out. "I need to go to the hospital."

"Okay, sure."

His mind raced as he searched for possible answers.

"Clint?"

"Ahh—sorry about that." He ran his fingers through his hair. "I'll take you out for lunch. Um—I just—I need to…"

Layla squeezed his hand reassuringly. "It is fine, Clint, we'll talk later." She tiptoed and planted a kiss on his cheek.

Feeling relieved that she didn't seem to mind his sudden urge to explore the hunch that burned in his mind, he picked up pace after she left and marched straight to the treatment room. Everything looked good. The first two patients had already left. The third was due to come in ten minutes. Perhaps he was reading too much into this situation. After all, Warner could easily take off fifteen minutes in between appointments, but the rule was that he stayed behind to calibrate the accelerator.

Clint strode over to the machine and read the calibrations. He checked the charts and then rechecked the machine. Something didn't add up. As he glanced at the big machine, suddenly everything fell into place with a loud click. He knew why his patients were dying—and the man responsible was in the smoothie shop taking a break.

He fished his smartphone out of his pocket and punched in the seven digits. "Hey, Layla!"

"Hi, Clint."

"This might take longer that I thought."

"No worries."

"Thanks, Layla, I owe you one." He quickly ended the call; only one thought dominated his mind…get to the administrator and show him what he found. Finally, he could get rid of this demon and move on with his work. Rage burned in his heart as he thought about the innocent lives lost and the pain and regret the families had suffered through.

It would all come to an end.

Or at least, that was what he hoped for.

Chapter Nine

Breathe and trust that you can survive this too. Trust that this struggle is part of the process. And trust that as long as you don't give up and keep pushing forward, no matter how hopeless things seem, you will make it.~Daniell Keopke

A few weeks later, Layla and Clint sat on the same bench where they'd enjoyed the divine waffles. It was a good day. The breeze grew stronger as it whipped around their bodies, and the waffles were hot and tasty.

"I can't believe this nightmare is finally over."

"Which nightmare are you referring to?" he asked.

Layla couldn't help the grin that lifted her lips. He was right, of course. Over the past days, they went to hell and came back. She had to deal with the implications of firing her manager, pressing charges against him, and hiring a new one.

Much to her surprise, the modeling industry came to her full support. She was hailed by many as the hero. The bald bombshell with smarts. They liked that she took a stand for what she believed in and didn't dismiss his attempt as many might have done.

"Bryan is neck deep in trouble. The case is moving at a fast track, and I think that he'll go to jail, but the good news is that my new manager is very supportive and has already landed me a new deal— but..." She bit a piece of her waffle, knowing that Clint was waiting for her to finish the statement. "I turned him down." She giggled when she saw how his eyes widened. "I've decided to go ahead with my soap manufacturing dream."

"Woo-hoo!" He couldn't seem to contain his excitement. "That's great."

"I've actually signed on with another company that's already making soap. They'll launch a new brand in my name. I'll be the face of it as well as the Creative Head. We'll own it together and I'll get forty percent of the profits."

"Wow."

"Yeah, and it's all thanks to you."

He took a bite of his waffle and sighed with contentment. "Me? What role did I play in the life of this great creative genius?"

"When I saw you working so hard to overcome the obstacles that stood in your way and then win against all odds, I realized that the only way we can achieve something that's important is to give it our best." Layla took another bite. "And in order to do so, we have to start somewhere. She sighed. "I was actually talking about your quest to get to the bottom of this mystery. I'm sorry that you lost four of your patients because of Warner's negligence."

The pain that swirled in his eyes wasn't new.

She knew that he would beat himself about the fact that he didn't latch on to the truth before the kids died. It wasn't his fault, but he was the one who was going to suffer.

"He has been fired and is facing serious charges regarding gross negligence, but it's not going to bring those kids back. Mark assured me that they've decided to take swift action. From a PR point of view, it looks good that they caught the person on their own and removed him before he could do more damage."

Layla frowned. "They didn't catch him. *You* did."

"Well, that's not the story that's going to the media." He shrugged his shoulders. "But who cares? It's not going to change anything."

She held his hand and squeezed it. "You did the best you could, Clint. Don't beat yourself about it."

He stood and tugged her hand. "Let's go and celebrate our victories at my place."

Layla's gaze was drawn towards the tall, distinguished man who was striding towards her. "Gage? What are you doing here?"

He took in her appearance. With the new wig, Layla looked the same as she did before. "I was walking past when I saw you."

All of a sudden, Layla felt overheated. "Um…" She turned to Clint. "Clint, this is Gage Shelton, my ex-fiancé."

"Ex?" Gage snorted. "Now that you've found a new guy, I've become your ex?"

"What are you talking about? You were the one who dumped me." She felt astounded at his audacity. What the hell was he playing at? "Are you suffering from amnesia?"

"Whatever, darling. I passed by your apartment and didn't find you." Gage cocked his head to the side. "Guess you're too busy to talk, huh. Models? My mother was right." His lips curled. "I shouldn't have trusted you. Never mind." He shook his head in what seemed like disgust. "See you around…or perhaps never."

Layla's mouth hung open as she watched Gage walk away. Had he lost his mind? Why did he say such terrible things? She turned towards Clint and saw the speculative gleam in his eyes. Suddenly, Gage's rant made perfect sense. He intended to create trouble between her and Clint. Did he stumble on the idea when he saw them together or did he actually find her to make Clint think she was two timing? "He's lying."

Clint rubbed his jaw as he stared at her. "He said he didn't break up with you."

"He's talking nonsense. We broke up because he didn't want to be with me. It was his decision, and to be honest, I was happy with it."

"Did you break up with him after you met me?"

"That's not true."

Clint didn't look convinced.

She couldn't believe that he would fall for such an obvious ploy by the man who was deliberately doing this to make mischief.

"I just remembered that I've got some loose ends to tie up at work." He strolled off before she could say anything.

Damn it! Layla couldn't believe that he would simply take whatever Gage said at face value. Didn't he realize she wasn't that kind of a person? She wasn't the sort to play games and cheat on people. Rather than try to stop him, she took a cab and went home. If he didn't believe her, then she didn't want anything to do with him. She couldn't possibly be with a man who didn't trust her implicitly.

Back in her apartment, she felt depressed. Rather than wallow in the misery of her love life, she focused on her work. Opening her laptop, she began to work on her program for her soap business. She had to give details to the company with which she was now a partner.

For several hours, she worked on the proposal and finally, satisfied with the work, she emailed it to them. Just as she finished sending it, her doorbell rang. Thinking it might be Clint, she opened the door. She glowered at the man who stood there. "Gage. What do you want?"

"Can we talk?"

"I don't think there's anything left to say."

"Yes, there is."

She didn't like the determined look on his face. Layla considered slamming the door in his face but instead, she stepped aside to let him. "Okay. Come in."

He walked inside, looked around as if he expected to see Clint, and then visibly relaxed. "I'm sorry about what happened today. When I saw you, I lost my head. You looked so beautiful."

"And you wanted me back, huh?"

He cringed at the harsh tone of her voice. "We were together for two years, Layla. It's not a short time."

"And yet, you didn't think about it when you dumped me because I was losing my hair." She pulled off the wrap she'd draped elegantly around her head. Her head was as bald as a coot. She'd hated to see the patches of hair like a barren desert on her head, so she opted to just keep her hair completely shaven. In fact, having a bald head wasn't low maintenance; it was no maintenance. She silently laughed at her wacky sense of humor over a situation that she'd once thought was the death knell of her career. "I'm still the same ugly girl, Gage. Are you sure you want this?"

He paled visibly. "I—we can get past this. What did the doctors say? I'm sure they can treat it."

Walking over to the door, she opened it. "There's nothing you can say that will ever convince me that I should get back with you. It's over, and it's going to stay that way."

He looked torn between his desire to make amends and his need to run away. "But—"

Suddenly, a wave of laughter bubbled over to the surface. She guffawed so hard, her ribs hurt. She stole a glance at him, and the sight of his reddened face made her experience another fit of laughter that left her breathless.

He glared. "Are you insane?"

She sucked in her breath, trying to control the laughter, but failing miserably.

"What's wrong with you? You're totally..." He flexed his fingers; his eyes cold and hard.

Layla swallowed her laughter. "You know what, Gage?" She felt the sudden need to get this ass out of her apartment and out of her life for good. "Getting alopecia was the best thing that happened to me, because it helped me to see who you really are. And to be honest, I don't like you...Not. One. Damn. Bit." She opened the door even wider. She couldn't wait to see the back of him. "Just go!" She didn't even care if he wanted to get back with her, despite the obvious 'disease' she was suffering from. Whatever he said wouldn't be enough to make up for the hurt he caused her.

Without another word, he marched out.

She closed the door and sighed with relief. The man was nuts. Why would she want to take him back? He dumped her once, and he could do so again. She wasn't going to take that chance. Instead, she was going to live her life on her terms.

She went to bed. Images of Clint flashed through her mind. Would he still accuse her of cheating on Gage with him? Frankly, she was done with men who didn't respect her enough. If he didn't believe her, she wasn't going to explain herself. No siree.

She didn't want to lose Clint, but if he didn't come around, she didn't have another option.

Dammit! Who am I fooling?

~* * * *~

Layla had just wrapped the bath towel around her body after stepping out of the shower when she heard the doorbell ring. If it was Gage, she was going to call security. She was done with that man. He couldn't keep barging into her life as if he owned it. Wrapping a towel around her head, she rushed to the bedroom and quickly donned a pair of cut-off jeans and a well-worn, white t-shirt. She jogged to the front door, amidst the impatient buzzing of the doorbell. Layla gasped, her heart racing.

Clint stood at the door, looking handsome as ever. "May I come in?"

Layla eyed the bouquet of white tulips he held in his hands and then him. "Sure." She stepped back, giving him room to enter.

He walked in and handed the flowers at her. "Layla..." He cleared his throat. "It was stupid of me to doubt you. Of course that man was lying."

She folded her arms and narrowed her eyes. "And what made you finally come to that conclusion?" She would be damned if she made things easy for him.

"You've been nothing but honest and forthright with me, and those things are what I love most about you." He shook his head, as if he couldn't believe how foolish he'd been to believe the worst of her. "I was jealous—insecure..."

"Gage came by yesterday. He wanted to get back with me."

He pushed his hand through his hair. "What did you tell him?" Clint sucked in a deep breath and then expelled it with a gush.

"I told him..." Layla stared at Clint for several seconds. It seemed as if he dreaded the answer. She couldn't bear to prolong their agony any longer. "I told him to get lost." She waltzed over to Clint and draped her arms around his waist and rested her head on his chest. She still held the tulips in her hand.

Clint wrapped his muscular arms around her body. His firm, strong heartbeat was reassuring. She wished she could stay in his arms forever, but she needed to give him a response. Layla raised her head and gazed up at him. His dark gaze looked troubled.

"How can I get back with him when I'm with you?"

"Do you forgive me?"

Emotions, hot and strong, swirled in the depths of her heart. Forgive him? A man who could so readily accept his mistakes was number one in her world. "Of course, I do."

A look of pure relief crossed his face. "I don't have an excuse except that I'm plain crazy about you. I love you, Layla."

She unwrapped her arms from around him and bent her head, inhaling the scent of the tulips. She headed over to the counter and placed the flowers in an empty vase, all the while glancing at Clint and hoping he could read all the love she felt for him reflecting in her own eyes. Then she sashayed back over to him and embraced him. "I love you more, Clint."

His arms encircled her waist and his lips descended on hers.

His tongue twisted with hers and she felt happiness course through her veins. She'd been nothing but lucky to have him in her life. He was the right man for her, the only one—and she wasn't stupid enough to let him go. Wrapping her arms around his neck, he deepened the kiss. He bent, and swooped her in his arms effortlessly. He then waltzed to her bedroom, with nary a protest from her.

She wanted this.

This was exactly how she imagined their love story would be. Perhaps there were a few hiccups in between but at last, they'd gotten to the right place. He lay her down on the bed. For a few moments, their gazes remained locked together.

Then he unbuttoned his shirt and shrugged it off.

Her mouth salivated at the sight of his gorgeous body...truly a delight to look at. Mimicking his movements, she slipped out of her t-shirt. After unclasping her bra, she tossed it aside. The gleam of appreciation that sparked in his eyes gave her the boost to go on. She wriggled out of her cut-offs and panties. Now, naked, she lay spread out before him. After a brief moment of hesitation, she also took off her wig.

The fact that his expression didn't change told her she'd made the right decision. How could she not love a man who accepted and respected her for who she was? There were no false notes with Clint. This was pure music, loud, clear, and uplifting.

He took off the rest of his clothes.

Layla couldn't wait for him to join her, for their bodies to entwine—to feel him pounding inside her. Putting her hands on the bed, she leaned back and he straddled her. When his head bent and his mouth captured her nipple, a low moan escaped her lips.

Flaming hot loops of passion skidded along her skin while he caressed and fondled her hard buds. One by one, he paid homage to each breast while she shuddered under him. Delirious with need and passion, she arched her back.

Yes...exactly what she wanted.

While his tongue brought her to the edge of insanity, his fingers flicked over her skin. Slowly, his hand travelled down until he reached the curls that nestled between her thighs. His thumb brushed over her sensitive nub. A storm of passion swept through her.

She writhed under him. Her fingers speared through his hair and she held on while he pleased her. His finger moved in and out of her satiny center. The orgasm that rippled through her was wild and powerful. Her body jerked beneath him.

He gave her a few moments to recover before his knee nudged apart her legs. She was already hungry for more. He hovered over her for a few seconds. She sucked in a breath and he ploughed his way into her. They were joined together—and it was a beautiful moment. She loved it. Her muscles clenched as her sheath stretched to accommodate him. He stroked in and out, and she enjoyed it. The need for release began to build inside her. Her gaze remained fixed on his face while he pounded into her with enough force to make her squeal. A low rumble escaped his lips as he fought to find his own bliss. They moved in perfect unison. The passion carried higher and higher on the squall that overtook each nerve.

It became too much.

She couldn't take the exquisite torture anymore.

A second orgasm rippled through her while she shuddered and screamed. Her back arched, and her body jerked.

He exploded inside of her. Even in this desperate moment, he remembered not to crush her with his weight. Instead, he kept his elbows on the bed and hovered over her.

This is real love—and she was luckiest woman in the world.

Epilogue

The right people are going to recognize your worth. They are going to respect you, appreciate you, and accept you, without forcing you to compromise who you are. Life is too short, and your happiness is far too important, to make room for anyone who treats you otherwise. ~Daniell Keopke

Three years later...

Layla and Clint linked hands as they strolled on the pavement of the lush and green Central Park on a beautiful summer day. The sun shone high on the sky, and a brisk wind blew.

"Liam," she called to their son who was twirling his body around in circles in the garden area.

Hearing her voice, he stopped and fell onto the grass.

"Come back here," she called with laughter in her voice.

He stood, wobbled for a moment, and then ran towards them. "Mama!"

Her heart clenched with joy. When she looked at him, she could see the shiny black hair she used to have and Clint's rich, dark-brown eyes. It was a mesmerising combination. Such a beautiful child, or perhaps she thought so, because he was hers.

Theirs.

It was hard to believe that she'd been blissfully married for almost two and a half years. Her son was just over a year old and already, he could say a few words.

Charlotte swooped him into her arms and twirled him around. The little girl had been a steady part of their lives ever since she'd met Layla at the hospital.

Liam's gurgling laughter echoed in the park.

"He loves it!" Charlotte exclaimed.

"Oh yeah, he does." Layla put her arm around Charlotte's shoulders when she finally stopped spinning Liam around. "But better make sure he doesn't get dizzy."

"Where are we going?" said Charlotte as she handed the toddler over to Clint. She'd been babysitting for them ever since Liam was born. It was actually just an excuse for them to keep tabs on the preteen who was growing up fast. The bond Layla shared with her didn't dim in all this time. In fact, it strengthened.

"We're going to the waffle shop." Layla winked. "Clint loves that place."

"It isn't just me," he protested. His gaze settled on his wife. "You love it too."

"Well, why shouldn't I? That's how our love story started. You, me, and the waffle cart," she countered. "I'll never forget those days."

"Well, let's see what the fuss is all about," Charlotte stated as they strolled to the waffle shop. The cart was long gone and the man now owned his own place. "It's good to get out of the house." She rolled her eyes. "Mom is all about the wedding, the gown, the menu...*arrgh*...and I want to pull my hair out!"

Layla laughed as she sank into a booth.

Clint got a highchair for Liam and settled him in. He headed over to the counter to place their orders. "It's generally like that with women when they are getting married. One day, you'll do the same."

"Ugh! I never want to get married," she claimed.

"Hear, hear!" Clint stated as he delivered the waffles.

They settled to eat. The waffles were as good as ever.

Layla snuck Liam a few pieces even though he wasn't supposed to eat sweets. "Now, you'll be getting a new stepfather. It will be cool."

Charlotte huffed. "He's okay, not that bad, but if I had a choice, I would rather have you guys as parents, step or otherwise."

"That's so sweet, darling, but we're always here for you. Always." Layla glanced over feeling pride for the preteen whom she considered as her own. She likened the relationship she and Charlotte had with the kind of relationship she always wanted to have with her own mother, Mary—but never really had. "You can count on us."

"I know I can." They finished eating. As they stood, Charlotte put her hand on Layla's arm. "That waffle was as good as advertised."

"Glad you liked it."

They stepped out of the shop. It was now a glorious evening.

Charlotte smiled. "Love how you wrapped your head, Layla. Suits you."

"Thanks, darling." She put Liam in his stroller.

Clint bent next to her, to help her strap in the toddler who was already rubbing his eyes. "You look hot, you know," he whispered, "I love you." He planted a kiss on her cheek.

She grinned as she gazed at her son and then into her husband's loving eyes. "And I. Love. You."

Love was in the air—and Layla was the happiest woman in the whole, wide world.

THE END

About the Author

Thank you for taking a chance on *THE DOCTOR'S SURPRISE PRESCRIPTION* and trusting me to give you a few hours of reading pleasure. I'd be happy if you do me a favor. Many potential readers depend on honest reviews to determine if they should 1-Click a book. Please help them make an informed decision by posting a review of *THE DOCTOR'S SURPRISE PRESCRIPTION*. Your review doesn't have to be long.

I love hearing from readers, so you may shoot me an email to author.roxywilson@gmail.com. That's how our friendship will begin, if we aren't friends already.

I also hope you'll consider joining my mailing list. By doing this, you'll receive updates on my upcoming releases, giveaways, deals and free reads. It will surely be an honor if you decide to subscribe. To join my mailing list, visit https://dl.bookfunnel.com/zv2wi4w57y.

Kind regards, always!
Roxy

Books by Roxy Wilson

Second Chance Romance:

Alessandro Mancini
Friends to Forever
Meant to Be

Holiday Romance:

Be With You: A Valentine's Romance
A Holly Jolly Christmas (Merry Matrimony, Book 1)
The Gift of Maggie (Merry Matrimony, Book 2)
Wynter Wonderland (Merry Matrimony, Book 3)
Loving St. Nick

Secret Baby/Pregnancy Romance:

A Lesson in Love
The Law of Love
Baby Wanted (A Bundle of Joy, Book 1)

The Baby Proposal (A Bundle of Joy, Book 2)
Baby, You're Mine (A Bundle of Joy, Book 3)
Secret Baby Seduction (A Bundle of Joy, Book 4)
This Time, Baby (A Bundle of Joy, Book 5)

Shapeshifter/Paranormal Romance:
Greer's Alphas
My Guardian Vampire
Bree's Purr-fect Mate
Nya's Wolf: BBW Paranormal Shape Shifter Romance
Fur-ever Yours: A BBW Paranormal Shape Shifter Romance (The Protectors Volume 1)
Fur-ever Yours: A BBW Paranormal Shape Shifter Romance (Volumes 1 & 2)
Fur-Ever Yours: A BBW Paranormal Shape Shifter Romance (The Protectors Book 2)
My Guardian Vampire, Volume 1

Cowboy/Western Romance:
Just Gettin' Started: BWWM Interracial Cowboy/Western Romance (Westbury Ranch, Book 1)
Stay With Me: BWWM Interracial Cowboy/Western Romance (Westbury Ranch Book 2)

I Only Have Eyes For You: BWWM
Cowboy/Western Romance (Westbury
Ranch Book 3)

Other Books:
BRUISED (An MMA Fighter Romance)
Take This Ring
Training Her Curves

Boxed Sets:
Baby Love Volume 1
Baby Love Volume 2
Yuletide Love Volume 1
Yuletide Love Volume 2